The Lights

The
Lights

The Lights

a novel by

BRIAN McGREEVY

THIS IS A GENUINE BARNACLE BOOK

A Barnacle Book | Rare Bird Books
453 South Spring Street, Suite 302
Los Angeles, CA 90013
rarebirdbooks.com

FIRST TRADE PAPERBACK ORIGINAL EDITION

Set in Minion Pro
Printed in the United States

10 9 8 7 6 5 4 3 2 1

Publisher's Cataloging-in-Publication data
Names: McGreevy, Brian, 1983-, author.
Title: The Lights : a novel / by Brian McGreevy.
Description: First Trade Paperback Original Edition | A Barnacle
Book | New York, NY; Los Angeles, CA: Rare Bird Books, 2017.
Identifiers: ISBN 9781945572128
Subjects: LCSH Dating—Fiction. | Family—Fiction. | Man-woman
relationships—Fiction. | Mothers and daughters—Fiction. | Austin
(Tex.)—Fiction. | BISAC FICTION/General.
Classification: LCC PS3613.C497245 L54 2017 | DDC 813.6—dc23

For Jim Magnuson

Birds born in a cage think flying is an illness.

—Alejandro Jodorowsky

hogwarts

Dear You,

THE SPRING OF THE dead birds, the one after
the death of my mother, I knew a broken
angel was going to come into my life. And
not a moment too soon! For a while after
the funeral people didn't know what to say
to me, and my presence made them uneasy, like a vaguely
defective appliance they were afraid of breaking. People don't
like thinking about these things, and yet won't believe you if
you tell them that quite literally nothing they can say has any

impact on the situation so it would be preferable all around for them to treat you normally without thinking about it all. Which is not to suggest normalcy is any kind of prize. I was working as an editorial assistant at a monthly culture magazine of some repute—working for *the* such and such, sufficiently inflating you in the eyes of others to divert you from the feeling of, on your better days, the triviality of your position and, on the average ones, an obscure but inexorable sense of doom. This, however, is why bars were invented: the carrot incentivizing you to lunch, and then happy hour, and, after the vice in your chest has finally relaxed, you're just sitting there like everyone else, dumber and drunker and waiting for something new to happen. Then the season turned and the birds came back, and the third or fourth time I found one fallen on my stoop to or from work, head askew and legs sticking up like a stem with all the grapes picked off, I got the point: it was in the wind, everything was about to change.

I didn't tell Mark. We were living together in a small walk-up on 126th Street and he was working at a corporate video-editing job worse than mine—at least I worked for *the* such and such—and he hated disruptions of the status quo. Like, for instance, a conversation about what had happened to his ambition to be a filmmaker, or how his fatalism had grown to the level that I would come home to find him miserable in a sweltering centrally heated apartment because he couldn't summon the will to get up and open a window. Or how often I was falling asleep before ten, fully clothed, with wine-stained teeth. Or how long it had been since it had occurred to me to be anything but fully clothed around him. So there was no point in upsetting him until there was, or until he noticed I was hiding something. Which he wouldn't.

I'm being FEARLESS, this is the point of this whole exercise. It is the first step in abandoning someone I loved. Or someone who loved me. Separating the two has never been my strong suit.

But you already know that.

Bear with me, baby. I am using my own words. The benevolent cult of which I am now a member encourages this approach, employing TACT and COMMON SENSE over its own potentially alienating jargon: *one day at a time, Higher Power, hitting your knees.* (Though I suspect you would have no objection to the last one, you autistic pervert.)

Then I got the letter informing me of my acceptance to Hogwarts. This was the very elite, prestigious, etc. graduate program in writing to which I'd applied. This had been an ambivalent decision. For starters, I could hardly think of four dumber words in the English language than "graduate program in writing." In this life some people have a destiny and some don't. It is as cruel and true as the inequality of love. And people with a destiny are not supposed to go to the Pharisees to learn it; the academy was not the sort of environment where the axe to break the frozen sea within us would be found. I believed as much as I believed anything that it was my destiny to *be* that axe. To the chagrin of copy editors, unfailingly spelling "axe" with an "e" was merely one proof of my literary seriousness!

But there were other considerations. The impossibility of things going on as they were, the impossibility of overcoming my fear of changing them by myself. There is a particular satisfaction THE REAL WORLD takes in reducing your formerly incandescent potential to a small set of numbingly proscribed paths. This process is a spectator sport in the rust belt city of which I am a native, and a familiar one to the recovering Catholic school pathological overachiever who could not repress the instinct to prove her worth, arm fluttering desperately with the RIGHT ANSWER, despite seeing in the sisters' faces how keenly they awaited her comeuppance.

So while the acceptance to Hogwarts (as I had taken to referring to the program during the application process, its reduction to adolescent fantasy a preemptive strike against my own fear of rejection) was to my thinking nothing more than a mirage that led in any direction but here, it was no less imperative to follow. It is a received part of the Galvan family oral tradition that I was born with one foot in this world and one in the next, and a chorus of dead birds is nothing to sneeze at.

Mark was predictably rattled. It meant moving across the country, and to central Texas, which as anyone from the Northeast knows is not a real place. But nothing else would be required of him than to be there and contain whatever would happen if I was left alone too long. Both of us should have been more worried about his commitment to this role. At social gatherings during our last couple of weeks in the city he would say, "She's the lightning and I'm the bottle." There was pride in his voice when he said this.

We arrived in Texas in August. South of Waco we stopped at a rest area with sweat puddles in dark stains on the backs of our legs even with the air conditioning on high. We looked out at flats of grass as yellow a shade of green it seemed like a living thing could be and still be a living thing. I said the heat was like a theological argument. Mark said it was too hot to be clever. We moved into a bungalow in east Austin. At the time the east side was in the early phase of serious gentrification, consisting of a mix of poor black or Mexican families and grad students and young musicians whose dart landed here on the map instead of Portland or Brooklyn. There were hipster coffeehouses with year-round Christmas lights and competing piñata stores and the cicadas were a wall of sound that seemed like it would close in at any minute. It seemed like every old man came out of the same mold: comically skinny posterior, beer belly that tapered to a point. I bought boots from a store where the sales staff wore deputy badges as name tags, the smell of leather reminding me of trying on shoes from my mother's closet as a young girl.

My first weeks were spent mostly alone. Mark had found a nearly identical job and though he could have deferred starting he said he wanted to dive into routine. Both of us knew this wasn't the case: the trip down had occurred without emotional eruption from me and he didn't want to test his luck. It had been so long since I'd had time to myself that I was at a loss over what to do with it. Of course, drinking, but like the ticking of a clock this was hardly separable from the passage of time itself. When I did not have time for my own work, I desired nothing more, and now that I had it, I spent it on dysmorphia. I started running five- and seven-mile loops on the trail around the river in the heavy, wet heat. By the end my clothes were soaked through as though I'd been caught in a rainstorm and my eyes stung from the salt. My heritage is substantially Sicilian peasant stock, so my frame is small and my hips are broad and muscle packed easily on my thighs. I would make Mark encircle them with his hands and flex proudly like men do with their biceps when they come back from the gym. One day on the trail I was caught in an actual rainstorm. I had never experienced anything like a storm in central Texas. Its advent was sudden and without warning and all around me water pounded the earth with a force that bordered on the erotic. I made my way to a portable toilet off the trail and waited inside. The sound of the rain on the plastic walls rattled my shinbones. Then, just as suddenly, it was over, and by the time I got home there was no black in the sky and the heat had sucked all the wetness off the pavement and there was no reasonable argument to be made that it had rained in the first place. I noticed an urgent fluttering of white, tissue-like paper in my path, though there was no breeze. I crouched. It was two butterflies on the sidewalk in a state as biblical as the storm. I was breathless at the defiant fragility of this coupling, which I could not believe any boot or atomic weapon could bring harm to. It was then that I realized the truth, that East Coast elitism had nothing to do with it: Texas was not a real place—like the heart it could be located in space and time, but its most essential coordinates could not. Living here was as like living inside a beautiful and melancholy and possibly fictitious memory as it was actually happening.

✦

THEN THE TERM STARTED and stillness gave way to a blur of orientations and receptions and introductions, introductions, introductions. Though I would have sooner swallowed hot coals than say so, I had been terrified of meeting the other students at Hogwarts. Its exceptional funding ensured its exclusivity, and on paper everyone was outrageously accomplished: Harvard and Yale grads, former Stegners and Fulbrights, a poet or two I had actually seen in respectable literary magazines. I imagined them looking at my BA from the not-quite-Ivy arts college that wore its mind-blowing pretentiousness and self-satisfaction to mask its secret shame as a safety school, and my position at *the* such and such, which they would be with it enough to understand the actual loserdom of, and my ears boiled. But reality disappointed, and everyone was nice enough.

What a moronic fraudulence. Everyone was certainly not NICE ENOUGH; this is the worst Pollyanna lie to evade the pulpy heartbreaking screaming person-ness of everyone around you at any moment, but all of this was a thousand years ago now when we were made of the ideas we had about ourselves and not the choices yet to be made and it is the simple and unbelievably lonely truth that almost all of the people around you at any moment are background actors. This isn't about them. It's about us, baby, and we are no more relevant to them, unimaginably.

Either way, there were two glaring exceptions. Take an academic situation based on the mutual assumption of our elevation over the base considerations of the MARKET, while not so secretly fueled by the crass desire for validation by the same, and this is the exact kind of brittle veneer it is irresistible for a certain kind of adolescent ego to shatter. These two egos were Harry and Jason, and I hated them both immediately. Harry was the worse offender. He was prone to sweeping assertions that symbolism had no place in the short story, or that he would never write anything with an iPhone in it. In addition, he had spent a decade working in advertising, giving him a messiah complex. He believed that his soul had undergone privations in corporate America that the rest of us could not be expected to understand, as well as a practical comprehension of THE REAL WORLD that he would communicate in disgruntled sighs when conversation took a turn for the naïve or theoretical, followed by a suitably masculine and condescending lecture on how things actually worked. His writing consisted of the hardscrabble sufferings of blue collar Idahoans, although he had grown up in this region a child of what he held in greatest contempt: the classroom. Both his parents had been professors more conversant in squabbles over parking spaces in the faculty lot than scavenging a house for copper wiring. He was heavily tattooed and had one cauliflower ear and was just below average height for a woman, which he compensated for with a caricaturesque musculature and by hating women, though he attempted to disguise the latter in the form of reductive and aphoristic humor. He considered himself Faulknerian in his understanding of people's inner workings but never came to a more nuanced evaluation of gender politics than *women be shoppin'*.

Jason, his familiar, suffered from the same testosterone poisoning that led to the belief that crassness was the better part of valor, but his case was less straightforward because Jason was a child. Looking back, it is unbelievable to me what a child he was. At the first couple of functions I noticed him at I didn't notice him at all, really, assuming he was some faculty brat exploiting the free sparkling wine. And despite my skepticism of Hogwarts as an institution, my response upon discovering he was a student was one of indignation: who let this child in here! This tedious golden child. He was a long, sandy blond Texan, baby-faced and blue-eyed in a thirties matinee idol sort of way as though to bludgeon the world with his favored genetic inheritance. He dressed in blue jeans and Lucchese pointed toe boots regardless of the heat, a boy rebelling against the boyishness of shorts. I was to discover he looked so young because he was; he had come into the program straight out of undergrad and had had the gall to finish undergrad early. To be sure, I have never been any sort of advocate for the cult of LIFE EXPERIENCE, only confirmed by meetings of my benevolent cult sitting on metal folding chairs in church fellowship halls listening to men and women who have lived hard, bad lives but possess no voice to tell about them outside of the most maudlin platitudes— but the fact of this child's existence still rankled me. The biography of an artist is of interest only to an artist judging herself in comparison, and such is the myopia of competitive anonymity that relative youth seemed like a thing worth getting bent out of shape over. When, of course, there was only one relevant question that wasn't openly discussed but nevertheless changed the molecules of the air like a high-tension wire. And this was: which of us would MAKE IT— while knowing that, statistically, most would not, and silently sizing up, envying, cursing, and praying about who among us were God's Favorite Children.

Not even Harry and Jason were defiant enough to talk about this out in the open, but it was no surprise to me to later discover that they did so in private, with the kind of detail and morbidity that girls use to talk about their bodies—analyzing the self-defeating flaws in other people's work/thought/character while using terms like *data point* and *brand management.* No epithet offended them more than "writer's writer," believing fame to be simply a form of attainable capital. Either your goal was to become famous or you were a liar. They liberally punctuated these conversations with quotes from man movies. "Coffee is for closers. Fuck you, pay me." These were the qualities they believed separated them from the rest of Hogwarts, but the one that probably did so the most was that being here never made them feel safe: in what was intended as a place of artistic sanctuary they always felt like the wolves were at the door. But they were the wolves, two crude alpha wannabes who mistook their basest instincts for metaphysical assumptions about aristocracy.

A week or two into the term there was at a kickoff barbecue that was held at a small ranch house to the southwest of the city amid an expanse of hills of sage and cedar and prickly pear. I drank mint juleps and basked in the praise of professors who were on the admissions committee and happily answered questions about my "influences," taking care to omit *contemporary fiction.* Though I had had misgivings about going back to school, I had always been good at it. It's a sort of reversion to childhood when corresponding to a simple set of expectations results in being treated with the importance of a thoroughbred. My own childhood consisted of praying nightly that the cocktail of alcohol and benzos would hit my mother only after the lit cigarette had extinguished in her hand and not on the couch and carrying my asthma medication with me in my backpack so I didn't have to fear one of her friends going through my things and stealing it—I flourished in the structure and predictability of school.

When I finally tired of Lisa Simpson–ing, I went inside the ranch house to have a moment to myself and have a snoop, two of my favorite things. I was admiring the skulls and antlers and furs (like my mother, I had an intense appreciation for the aesthetification of death) when I was joined by Harry and Jason, the disparity in their size and body type, a fire hydrant next to a parking meter, calling to mind a Depression-era pair of tramps. In fact I was not "joined," I had been stalked. New females were objects of great interest at Hogwarts, and I had lost track at this point of the number of timid questions I had been asked about my CV or favorite *This American Life* episode by circling males. This was great fun, the most I'd had since having too much to drink at the magazine's Christmas party last year—the pleasure of reminding yourself you are a sexual being without the risks of doing anything about it. These two were not so subtle in their approach.

"How old are you and how much do you weigh?" Harry asked.

"Did you focus group that one at Wieden and Kennedy?" I replied.

"No, I think I used it on the first woman I talked to after my divorce."

"I can't imagine why it didn't work out."

"She got tired of being the big spoon," said Jason.

"Do you realize it's ten million degrees out?" I said. "You may as well be wearing Crock-Pots on your feet."

"Gotta pay the cost to be the boss," he said.

"How old *are* you?" I said. "Did you get a reference letter from your pediatrician?"

This was met with an inevitable banality about receiving one from my mother. They were pleased with themselves, imaginary Norman Mailers and George Plimptons toasting their defiant political incorrectness. I mulled the benefits of shaming them with my mother's death, but I was not interested in this becoming a real conversation.

"I'm underwhelmed, guys. I went to an arts college so I've seen the thing before where boys act like jerks because they think it makes them less gay. Side note: I know it's hot out, but I really don't think it's healthy for a human being to produce that smell."

The smell of Harry's armpits was almost comically intrusive and rank—"bestial," I would call it, if I didn't know what satisfaction he would take in it—if you sat too close to him or if he put his arm around you, as was often the case if you were a female and he'd had more than half a drink.

Harry lifted an arm and inhaled deeply as if into a bouquet of flowers.

"You're right, this is an unhealthy level of virility. But I have smelling salts in case you pass out."

"If I pass out of anything it's going to be boredom, but you probably get that from all the girls. What happened to your ear?"

"A bar fight," said Harry.

"Real people don't get into bar fights."

"They do when it's a question of dignity."

"How many times a day do you say that to Terry Gross inside your head?"

"I don't even get around to it, honestly. I'm too busy waving smelling salts under her nose. 'Damn these pythons, Terry! Why did I have to come in here on a full pump?'"

He flexed his arms in that way that heavily muscular men are looking for an excuse to do even under the auspices of joking.

"So what do you and Terry talk about after your first collection of Connecticut divorce fiction?" said Jason.

I poured my drink down the front of his shirt and left them to find another girl whose pigtails they could pull, but as I was walking out of the room I bumped into the evening's host, a portly, soft-spoken popular Texas historian. The property was a university-sponsored writers residency and this man was the current occupant. My inner Lisa Simpson could not waste an opportunity to suck up, so soon afterward the three of us were listening to him discuss the biography he was working on of famed Texas Ranger John Coffee "Jack" Hays. It was news to me there was such a thing as a non-athlete "famed Texas Ranger," but Harry was obviously excited for the opportunity to speak to a real author whose interests he didn't consider hopelessly effeminate (also, apparently Hays, one of the state's undisputed tough guys, was short). Harry demanded of the historian what guns he'd brought. The man said the residency had a strict no-gun policy. Harry scoffed, "bureaucrats," then insisted the man level with him. To Harry, who had once proudly proclaimed that whenever someone began a conversation about "the novel" he started thinking about guns, a person surrounded by this much undisturbed wilderness with no armory was unthinkable. The historian shrugged and adjusted his glasses uncomfortably.

"Cocksucker!" said Harry. "I knew I should have brought my crossbow. I thought about it, but I didn't. Goddamn it, any time you think you should bring your crossbow but you leave it at home you end up needing it!"

The historian agreed in polite bafflement.

"You can borrow mine if you want," said Harry. "I could drop it off. And my chainsaw. Think about how much better that view would be if you cleared some of that cocksucking cedar."

I fulfilled the obligation of my gender by gently steering the conversation into territory more congenial to our host, who did not suffer confusion as to the difference between his he-man subject matter and himself. I asked if his family missed him, it being such an inconvenient drive to the city.

"They'd probably be happier if I were in Fort Stockton!" he said with a chuckle.

Harry looked at me with disdain. He had been discussing matters of masculine interest and I had turned them to the domestic. I did not disagree with him; as much as the he-man act was like nails on a chalkboard for me, it made me feel small and womanly that I had made things more *safe*. But to annoy him even more I made my voice reedier and upturned and drew out the *sylla-bllllles* as I asked the historian more questions about his wife's interior design firm and his daughter's engagement and other things that the only person who could have cared less about than I did was Harry.

He tolerated this sullenly, eyes darting around the room in boredom, when uncontainable childlike exuberance overtook his face.

"Holy shit, do you know what this is?" he said.

He sprung to the mantle and picked up an object, a rusty old ranching tool that looked a little like a large nutcracker.

"This is called a Burdizzo tool. You put it around the scrotum and the jaws clamp down on the blood vessels," he said. "It kills the balls."

Harry advanced on Jason, jabbing the tool at his crotch and working the jaws.

"C'mere! C'mere, *bwah!*" said Harry.

Our host chuckled and shook his head in avuncular approval few men can resist of BOYS BEING BOYS.

"What a character," he said to me, and once again I coursed with resentment and envy at a man like Harry's continual ability to get away with being himself.

Later on, a few of us went out for a walk on one of the various trails. I wanted to pass; at this point I'd had a quite a few mint juleps and would have been far happier lying down for a nap in the shade, but it was too early in the term to be the uncharming drunk girl, and also Mark wanted to go and I knew he would not without me. When I'd rejoined him outside he already had that look of lost-child anxiety that he got when I left him alone too long at social functions. Of course Harry assumed role of scout leader: edifying us on the plant life we passed or the different bird cries, crouching to evaluate the freshness of a wild pig track (and once more cursing himself for not bringing a crossbow). He gestured at an expanse of hills.

"But this is nothing. There is a valley so wide in west Texas that if you yell 'git up!' and go to bed, eight hours later the echo will be your alarm," he said, mugging.

Mark smiled, which annoyed me. But it had been years, college, probably, since he'd had male friends, or really any friends other than me. *Don't be* that girl, *he is allowed to smile at whatever he wants to,* I told myself.

One intriguing takeaway from his lecture was Jason's lack of participation. His attention drifted, presumably from familiarity with the material but also, I was to learn later, genuine lack of interest. I will unfailingly find the fault line if it exists and was pleased to discover this one: Jason, like the historian, was a product of suburban Texas, and his interest in manly things was entirely theoretical—any hands-on attraction to guns or tools or which berries were poisonous substantially less than reading about it. Jason's distraction obviously caused Harry paternal disgruntlement, and this pleased me.

Is it possible Jason emerged so early as strategic terrain between Harry and me that could be manipulated? Maybe the facts that followed are inflecting what actually happened. But it is not impossible.

We reached a small collection of droppings on the trail. Harry crouched again to determine the species of origin. He took out his pocketknife and shaved off a sliver and with an intensely furrowed brow licked the blade.

I died.

I lay down on the trail and draped my arm over my eyes, unconcerned now about being the sloppy drunk girl. He was literally eating shit and I literally died.

"You probably don't want to lie down there," said Harry.

I waved my arm dismissively. "You win at nature. Congratulations. I'm having a nap."

"You really need to get up," said Mark.

I opened my eyes to glare at him, willing to be *that girl* in the face of this sedition. But I saw the genuine concern in his eyes before feeling a tingle on my bare legs, which shortly became a fiery stinging as I leapt up, wildly dancing and brushing off dozens of red ants.

As I write this now years later the sensation is no less vivid, not simply the pain of the stings but also the cool frisson that came just before, the numinous thrill of it.

two encounters

HAVING SOLIDLY ACQUIRED A reputation as the drunk girl who ended up in the emergency room (which I did not really mind, drama being a quality that far exceeds class in the Galvan hierarchy), my relationship with the two-man mutual appreciation society soon evolved with encounters I had with each individually.

The first occurred between Harry and me at group drinks after a lit class. His significant other was not in this class.

The topic of discussion—domestic novels—had continued to the bar and another classmate proposed that the most ideal subject of this genre was female infidelity, because it combined the maximum amount of conflict and interiority.

I considered this to be an interesting point, but was troubled by it. "Then why is it that the canonical novels about it are all written by men?" I asked.

Another classmate offered the simple explanation that the domestic novel achieved its peak in the nineteenth century, at which point female infidelity was such a controversial and threatening subject it could only be addressed by men.

Harry put his face in his hands, annoyed that we were discussing a fictional mode he was about as interested in as chewing light bulbs, and as long as we were on the subject still getting it wrong.

"The reason men are the ones who write about women cheating is because women lie about it," he said.

"I would have expected you to say the most unbelievably sexist thing in this conversation, and yet that was even more unbelievably sexist than I would have imagined," I said.

"It's not sexist, it's actually the opposite of sexist," he said. "You can't have compassion for something without trying to genuinely understand it."

"Please illuminate your superior *understanding* of my sex," I said.

"It's not that complicated," he said. "Four billion years of biological hardwiring has made women into lying machines."

I threw my hands up inquisitively to the group; was I hallucinating that this walking gland was actually saying these things?

"See, what you're doing here is looking at it with a *value judgment*. Your enlightened liberal brain has been programmed to react in certain ways to certain words, and your reaction is to get offended. Which, by the way, is the least interesting way to respond to any philosophical question."

He was lecturing *me* on the etiquette of philosophical discourse! He was a gland!

"Because there's no way a person might be offended on their own account at calling half the human beings on the planet 'lying machines.'"

"You really are staggeringly incapable of seeing your own programming right now. Peahens evolved earth-tone colors to hide from predators. This is a lie, camouflage is a lie, it is saying, 'I am not a thing for you to kill and eat, I am a mound of dirt.' By contrast, the peacock's baller coloring is saying A) 'come and get me bitches,' and B) 'the fact that I'm still alive means that you should pass on my pimp-ass seed.'"

"Great, we're at peacocks already," I said. "Was there any other pseudo-scientific theory that unbelievably sexist people use to prove the inferiority of women you wanted to cover?"

"Jesus Christ, evolution is not 'pseudo-science,' it's the definition of *science* science."

"You know there is no correlation between the length of your penis and the number of times you use the word 'science' to support your own argument?"

"True, though it's added like a hundred centimeters to the girth. But the subject here is not my powerful-yet-elegant Saxonate manhood—which by the way is a substantially more interesting conversation—it's why women are liars because of their smaller brains."

"Here we go!" I said.

"Again, I apologize that I didn't spend four years in a small arts college discussing Victorian-era lesbian poets, but if I can have a second to *elaborate* without you jumping down my throat with your *programmed* reaction. The female brain is roughly ten percent smaller than the male brain, but equal *mass*. This means that there is the same number of neurons but in the female brain there is a denser network of connections, giving men the advantage in compartmentalization and linear reasoning, but women a greater aptitude for multitasking and intuition. And woman, being the physically weaker and less aggressive sex, has to rely on her superior intuitive intelligence in a world where, for the majority of history and pretty much everywhere today below the poverty line, she is dependent on men for resources and protection. This is why, as a survival mechanism, women are genius and instinctive liars; so genius in fact that they have the power to *believe their own lies*, which is like Jedi level. Your boyfriend Tolstoy himself said he would tell the whole truth about women when he had one foot in the grave, then jump in. Obviously he was referring to the biological fact that it is a gender of little shoppers whose relationship to reality is like Israel and Palestine. Except Israel and Palestine are neighbors."

He swept his arm, flexing his tricep. "Look at people. We are a greedy, selfish, deceitful species. The simple explanation for this is sexual selection, because only males capable of getting around female's inability to be accountable or transparent about their own nature are reproducing! From the perspective of slave morality, that's a value judgment, but from a *scientific* perspective, it's simply an effective adaptation."

"Good," I said. "I'm glad you threw in a Nietzsche reference in case there was any question left about the deluded misogyny of your thinking."

"What does that even mean? I don't know what the word 'misogyny' means anymore except that the person you're talking to has probably stopped listening."

"It's actually a more polite way of calling you an asshole."

"Once again confirming your rote ignorance outside the arts, which is why ninety-nine percent of artistic work being produced today is trivial horseshit."

"You smell like your argument."

By now something had been released, something angry and brittle and in need of proving, lying behind what both of us were saying, fueled by alcohol and a politically volatile subject and the mutual identification that something inside both of us required this fight well before we'd ever met.

"Lemme ask you something," he said. We were standing outside on the patio and the physical distance between us had closed and a vein was throbbing in his head and he was aggressively jabbing with his index finger. Others in the party were making helpless attempts to defuse the situation but we ignored them.

"You ever cheat on anyone?" he said.

"No. I would never do that."

"Good for you," he said. "Well, I've been cheated on. In fact, I was publicly cuckolded by the woman I was married to. So *maybe* this is a subject I actually do know a thing about, and you don't, so my personal *experience* means a little more than your little-girl fantasies."

Things got a little red for me after that. There were more heated words and the predictable regression into schoolyard insults before we were successfully separated. At home that night I told Mark what had happened, and that Harry had screamed at me in front of a group of people, leaving out some of the choice things I had said to him.

"I really oughtta deck that guy," said Mark, almost convincingly.

✦

THE FOLLOWING SATURDAY THERE was a revival screening of an old film downtown. Mark was working and I could have tried to get any one of my bright and culturally literate new friends to come with me, but I didn't. I have a thing about seeing movies by myself. It's a perverse habit that I formed as a teenager, combining two of my great passions: going to movies and feeling voluptuously lonely. Of course every person with self-destructive tendencies also has a wildly sentimental streak, and even the worst movies hit me where I live. I got downtown early and stopped at a hotel bar before the show. It was the destination hotel of the city, where the wall sconces were pistols and there was art of Indian raids and brochures about the ways it was haunted. I was still in my infatuation phase with Texas and its self-unaware extravagance charmed and fascinated me. Jason was at the bar. He sat marking up a manuscript with a pen. We were in no classes together, and it was the first time I'd seen him outside of a group, much less detached from the love of his life. It came as a surprise to discover him here with an existence all to himself. He did not see me, and I spent a moment pretending to be annoyed at having my loneliness intruded on, before taking the stool next to him.

"Is it bad Denis Johnson or bad Cormac McCarthy?" I said.

He gave me a look.

"All boy writers are either doing bad Denis Johnson or bad Cormac McCarthy," I said.

He angled the manuscript toward me. It was a screenplay. I didn't know he was a screenwriter.

"I'm gonna be a pretty big thing in Hollywood," he said.

I was surprised to find this endearing. If he had made this sort of proclamation around the gland it would have gotten under my skin but, in contrast to the dangerous chip on Harry's shoulder, one-on-one Jason had a kind of sweet nervousness, a strain of adolescent apologeticism beneath the hubristic self-assertion, as well as an inability to sustain eye contact. It was unclear whether this was an essential difference or if Jason simply hadn't been living his own legend long enough to blur the distinction.

We talked about movies. This was a relief to me; by now I had exhausted myself trying to prove I had sophisticated things to say about literature. I was also intrigued by his baldly commercial ambition. Within a petri dish like Hogwarts there is a perceived honor to obscurity, and if you did have an attraction to a suspiciously accessible medium such as film it was typically with the aim of reducing its intrinsic populism, small coming-of-age dramas about sexual identity with endings too ambivalent to be considered unhappy, that sort of thing. Not so with Jason: he was like a cross-pollination between Pauline Kael and a twelve-year-old male.

"I want to tell heroic stories," he said. "I want to tell stories about heroic badasses slaying their enemies and banging awesome broads."

I gave him a dubious look, but could not actually disapprove of the ingenuousness of this admission. I also noted his use of the qualifier "awesome."

"So what's your movie about?" I said.

"It's sort of a combination of Sergio Leone and *Star Wars*."

"You just said so many things I don't care about in one sentence," I said.

I went to the bathroom and when I came back he resumed the conversation about his script as though there had been no interruption of his thought process.

"Are you, like, autistic?" I said.

"What the hell kind of thing is that to ask?" he said.

"You're really socially weird and bad at eye contact."

"What an asshole thing to say."

"I mean you're clearly on the spectrum."

"Yeah, probably."

I had another round and this turned into more than I intended, doing the thing where after one sip my elbow never extended more than forty-five degrees. I was feeling intrigued and sociable and in the mood for spirits. This mood also materialized when I felt the opposite. It was really only when drinking alone that my glass ever touched the tabletop, or with Mark.

Drunkenness suffused and Jason talked at length about the movie we were about to see, its context in the director's filmography, its antecedents and decedents. He was prone to *Rain Mansplaining*: an endless stream of words somersaulting over themselves. This got past my defenses because a person who talks too much is giving you stuff that they don't know can be used, because it doesn't occur to them that it can. I was having fun. Though I am a match for J. Edgar Hoover in my listening skills, it does not mean I enjoy it. Mostly I make my face hurt with forced smiles and, in my heart, grieve the God-shaped hole in what people think they care about. Jason was honest, rudely and entertainingly so, and when he talked about movies it was with a joy that lit his whole face.

"Underneath this whole act you're really just a big nerd," I said. "You probably quote *The Simpsons* on dates. I know for a fact you do."

"And underneath the Dorothy Parker thing you're an unmarried thirty-year-old from Pittsburgh your family probably thinks is a lesbian," he said.

I dipped my fingers in my drink and flicked them at him.

"I'm *twenty-six*. But I know all grown-ups just look old to you."

"Thank you for not throwing your drink at me," he said.

"I never threw my drink at you, I poured what was left of my drink on you. Which you should be grateful for because I really love throwing drinks at people when they have it coming, which you totally did."

"I recall what made you *pour* your drink on me and am still at a loss."

"You made an assumption. You assumed that I want to make small art."

"Well, what do you want to make?"

"Well, Terry, I want to write *blood*. The blood that rises in your cheeks when someone slaps you in the face while you're being fucked, that's what I want to write."

He thought about this. "Cool," he said.

"I actually don't know why I said that, Terry. I've been a serial monogamist since I was fourteen, and I've certainly never been slapped in the face while being fucked."

(I said it to settle definitively that I was not a LITTLE GIRL.)

"I guess half the shit we say is just to figure out whether or not it's true," he said.

We fell quiet and I regarded him, the unquestionable handsomeness of his face but the asexual quality it took on because of his youth and weirdness. Finding a new friend is a form of intoxication fundamentally unchanged since childhood, the giddy queasiness of it. New friends are the worst.

"I'm sure I will throw a drink at you one day, you're really annoying," I said.

We walked over to the theater together and sat together, and for the first half hour or so I couldn't concentrate. I was drunk and distracted by the feeling that all the things I wanted were within reach. The contrast of this feeling with my life just the previous spring would have been irreconcilable if reflecting on it seemed to have any relevance at all. Something about Jason inspired this feeling of wanton possibility; the bigness of his optimism and ambition made you feel that the ceiling of the universe was higher. I remember feeling this, though not what it actually feels like, in the same way it's impossible to remember the actual experience of pain. It's a small mercy. As I write this the Monongahela is black with blotches of white ice like a corpse victim to some frontier disease and the mercy of the day is its brevity, the early sunset bringing the relief of darkness, and everything I felt in that place seems as distant and impossible to return to as the place itself. Thinking of the early days in Texas can make me cry hard enough for my father to brave a soft knock on the door to make sure I don't do something that scares him even more than checking in on me.

By the end of the movie I was sober and sensible and we parted ways with the stilted formality of strangers who had over-shared, though we had spoken only of work.

"He feels bad, by the way," Jason said.

I pretended not to know what he was talking about.

"He told me you guys got into it. He knows he crossed the line and he feels bad about it."

"Is something keeping him from telling me that himself?" I said.

He had actually sent me an apology email the next day[1] but I hadn't informed anyone; there is an innate Galvan tendency towards martyrdom which includes unconsciously leveraging sympathy at every opportunity.

He shrugged. "I guess it's none of my business."

I was annoyed then at the inherent stupidity of innocence, this attempt at peacemaking introducing sourness to an otherwise enjoyable encounter. We stood awkwardly, both searching for the right note to end on. Then, on a whim, I

---

1   Dearest Sappho,
Sorry for being a jerk. It happens sometimes. You're alright for a big Sappho. SORRY! *hearts* —HVC

grabbed the script from under his arm, and walked a couple of blocks down and around the corner to the less convenient bus stop so we wouldn't end up going in the same direction.

✦

I READ JASON'S SCREENPLAY that night and it was a thing of beauty. The movie it made in my head was more vivid than the one I had just seen. The plot? Who cares. It was an archetype of old school Hollywood storytelling, operatic and suspenseful and romantic, even the smallest gestures a hundred times bigger than life, and everything as fraudulent and joyfully truthful as life ought to be. One line made me laugh out loud reading in bed. Mark did not ask me what, so I said "ha" to reiterate.

"I thought you thought this guy was a dick," said Mark.

"Yeah, but he's kind of a really good dick."

I had him read a few pages.

"Clever," he said. He was seventy pages into a screenplay he meant to shoot himself. A coming-of-age drama with an ambivalent ending. He'd been seventy pages into it for two years. I told myself I wasn't being cruel. I told myself it would help him to see people finish things.

the mythic dimension

THAT WEEK I DIDN'T run into Jason again, but the subsequent Saturday there was another film in the series and I went to the same bar beforehand. He was there. We both pretended this was a funny coincidence. He didn't ask me if I'd read it. I didn't tell him he was right: he would be seeing his name in lights. I was excited for him, the way it is always exciting to meet a person with a destiny. We talked about the Bechdel test. Jason was of the mind that this was the worst kind of condescending East Coast elitism.

"It's a free market," he said. "Basically the argument is that women in fly-over states should want more enlightened things."

I pointed out that we had a culture to enjoy as a result of East Coast elitism.

"This is the Republic of Texas," he said. "Kindly hang your colonialist horse shit at the door."

I pointed out that he and Harry were two of the most elitist people I ever met; they were constantly self-referring as "the boss" or "the king" or equivalent inflating parlance that could only be interpreted as performance art except neither of them were kidding.

"Real people don't go around calling themselves 'the king,'" I said.

"You have this weird obsession with what real people do," he said. "Put it this way. My favorite book as a kid was *The Macmillan Book of Greek Gods and Heroes*."

I scoffed at the obviousness of this and respected him for ignoring it.

"My mom got it for me for Christmas in the first grade. It put me on the path. What I learned was the distinction between fiction and myth, and the distinction is that fiction is *fiction*. There are different planes of reality. The one we see is tedious and mundane and it's where most people spend every day half awake, with an underlying terror over their own insignificance. But there is another *mythic* plane that overlaps with the sort of lame one where life is both a personal experience and a symbolic act and you are the completely unfuck-with-able hero whose every step and setback and victory has cosmic implications—and the only difference between these two realities is *which story you tell yourself.*"

"So do you buy you-flavored Kool-Aid in bulk?" I asked.

"And the most important thing you can do in this moment is admit you're afraid you agree with every word I just said."

It was unusual for him to make direct eye contact and more than a little disconcerting. By temperament, and because his ego didn't need the help, I was compelled to take an adversarial stance against much of what came out of his mouth, while failing to bear in mind that even a person who talks too much can still be observant, that the way you withhold can be just as revealing as what they offer. I was surprised at how uncomfortable his look made me. The way he looked at you made you feel like you were the only thing in the world. I averted my eyes to my thumb worrying the sweat of my drink.

"I come from a place where being an inch taller than everyone else means they'll be waiting outside your door to cut you down to size," I said.

"Well you're in Texas now," he said.

"*Possibly*," I said.

✦

THE NEXT WEEK WE were in our now-customary spot immersed in our now-customary mode of conversation: impassioned, urgent, caroming from drink to drink and idea to idea, my elbow at that perpetual forty-five degrees. We were talking about our greatest fears. I was opening up to him. It's possible I didn't entirely mind being looked at like the only thing in the world.

Hers: DISTRACTION. The demon of her line, which consisted of a high incidence of addled brilliance and existential turbulence. This demon had come to plague her once in the form of the magazine, but there were any number of dumb, devious masks it might wear to get close enough to insert its proboscis and drain the best of you, the stuff that was supposed to go into the work. This was the perennial question of being a participant versus an observer. Was it possible to be both, meaningfully? Maybe for some, not for her. In her bones she knew her calling was to sit somewhere quiet and watch, like Buddha under the tree, while this seductive adversary did its worst. The things that happen to you before your real life starts, that usurp it. She had made an agreement with herself that if she was unmarried and unpublished by the time she was thirty, she would throw herself under a train.

"I have a suspicion you threaten to throw yourself under a train a lot more than the average person," he said.

His: the middle. He had been born middle middle class with a vertebral quirk inclining him to the firmament. A child, inevitably, of a librarian and a used-car salesman in post-Reagan suburbia, he had been raised in an environment of tract housing, diet sodas, and syndicated sitcoms. But he shared with his home state a native tendency toward bigness, attracting him to the monomyth, and its purest expression: the motion picture. Hitchcock, Scorsese, Coppola, men who wrote their dreams in light. The mass-manufactured disposability of the middle class fueled, rather than extinguished, the urgency of his mystical inquisitiveness; he spent his adolescence sharpening his wit with college students at Austin coffee houses and his bookshelf consisting of the trifecta of great twentieth-century religious synthesizers— Jung, Eliade, Campbell—as well as an unembarrassed collection of New Age self-help books—*The Intuitive*

Warrior, The Tools, The Way of the Shaman. Like Eliade he saw the New Age movement for all the stigma surrounding it as essentially positive: faith in the power of what can't be seen or measured, an affectionate optimism about the endless perfectibility of our species. Like Jung he not-so-secretly believed every word of it. A necessity, because the alternative was believing in suburbia.

I thought of my mother. When I was little, her worst insult was "mediocre." Her *favorite* insult was "cunt," but there was always a hint of admiration when she used it. When she called somebody "mediocre" it was like a ray that reduced another person to absolute nothingness. One day I asked her what it meant.

"When something is as far from being great as it is from being terrible," she said.

I realized I was telling him this, that I had inadvertently started talking about my mother with him. His face showed that he knew we'd entered precarious territory. His instincts, even then, directed him to be sensitive to my moods. I wanted to change the subject. Fate obliged. Abruptly he grew visibly tense: something had caught his eye and he averted his look, angling his body away from whatever he had seen.

"What?" I said.

"Group of suits by the piano," he said.

I looked over at a table of lawyer types, including one overweight young woman.

"Is she looking this way?" said Jason.

"What, did you bang her?" I asked, surprised. I expected a greater level of shallowness from him, and frankly would have been a little disappointed for this mystique to be dispelled.

He crinkled his nose. "What, *no*. Is she giving me the evil eye?"

"She hasn't seen you."

He slouched into his stool. "Tell me if she does. No, don't. I can't even deal with the evil eye, it makes me so uncomfortable you wouldn't believe it."

"You *rogue*," I said. "What did you do?"

"I briefly dated her friend. Her friend is much hotter, obviously. It became necessary to extricate myself from the situation, and it didn't go over well."

"What, did you Houdini?"

He shook his head in a jerky, Asp-y way. "Not clean. For one thing, it leaves the door open for when you're feeling lonely or another girl has shot you down or whatever to drunk-text her. And for another thing, it's unchivalrous. I told her I was engaged."

I looked at him skeptically.

"In this scenario, I'm the clear villain. She's not wondering if there's something wrong with her or confirming the general agitas women of a certain age can feel toward dating because this was an outlier of shittiness."

"You know it's way shittier to break it off with someone without giving them an honest explanation."

He defended himself. "So in this scenario she's working at a respectable law firm and doing pretty well, but is bored herself talking about work. One time after an all-nighter she goes into this Debbie Downer spiral thinking about how many hours of the last two days she's spent in the same ten-by-twelve-foot box, which she then starts extrapolating over the next forty years of her life. By the end of this conversation I want to slit my wrists with a butter knife. But it's a good income and she's got however much in student loans and this timetable for when she wants a house and kids and blah blah blah, all of these *notions* she has convinced herself are more important than being *free*. And it would have been unchivalrous to tell her we wouldn't be seeing each other anymore because *everything she's doing is wrong*."

"I don't believe that," I said. "If you're in a situation you can't see the way out of, you need to rise above it."

(So pleased with my own success with this transcendent function, I was blithely forgetting my doubt and fatalism the previous fall, Mark physically preventing me from deleting my Hogwarts application at the last minute.)

"Maybe you saying something about it would have given her the perspective she needed to do something," I said. "Maybe not and it would have haunted her forever like a drip in the next room. It's not for you to decide, and lying is never good juju, my friend."

It was unclear where my stance on this subject came from. I had been with the same person for seven years and the two boyfriends before that had gradually fizzled when we went to prep school and college, respectively. I'd never broken up with anyone in my life and could only attribute my sudden conviction to how pleasurable it was to disagree with Jason on anything because he was so obnoxious.

"Hold the phone!" I said. "What do you mean 'women of a certain age'?"

"She was twenty-eight."

I didn't know what offended me more: that this constituted "a certain age" or that he had dated someone older than I was. It was not impossible, of course, he was tall and objectively handsome, and in a distinguished graduate program. But it short-circuited my brain that an actual *woman* could take him seriously.

"You are probably the lamest person I've met in my whole life," I said. "And I *studied abroad*."

He didn't respond. A sort of rictus had overtaken his face and there was a trapped animal look in his eyes. I glanced back and saw that the woman by the piano had now seen him and was giving him the evil eye. Jason was not exaggerating how much this got to him, and I was to discover the formation of this anxious shell was his default response to things he found upsetting, a list which included but was not limited to: sustained eye contact, crowds, loud noises, or any kind of sensory overstimulation without the heavy use of intoxicants, having to use a ballpoint pen because his Pilot Precise had run out of ink, intense emotional exchanges when he wasn't in the mood, quotidian social exchanges when he wasn't in the mood, being touched anywhere near his Adam's apple, being late for movies (trailers emphatically *part of the movie experience*), and, perhaps most of all, any attempt to penetrate Fort Jason, which is what I came to call this retreat within himself.

I hit him. "Oh my God, *vomit*! She probably thinks *I'm* your fiancée!"

This was when I first learned how unamused he was by disruptions of Fort Jason, and also, in this moment of true vulnerability, how fun it was to torture him.

✦

MEMORY IS THE MURDERER of fact; good memory is genocide. In my mind this went on for weeks or months, our secret nonassignations—the hope I would pretend I didn't have to find him at the bar waiting and the pleasure when I would, the ranging conversations about what we considered to be crucially, redemptively true, at the theater buying sodas I had no interest in to accidentally graze his arm on the armrest...but innocently, the whole thing so funnily innocent that there was no reason to inform Mark, the whole thing so easily misread. In reality it only happened another one or two more times before Harry had to come in and wreck things for everyone.

Resentment speaking. Guarding the throne of self-deception is a Cerberus whose heads are self-centeredness, pride, and self-pity.

The truth: I'm using Harry as a scapegoat for my own lies.

The truth: he is still an ASSHOLE.

It was another after-class outing, our cohort congregated at adjoining picnic tables. Harry sat on one end holding court on something or other, likely making the other males feel inadequate by comparison. When Harry was out, there tended to be a gender segregation in the seating arrangement. Nevertheless, I was attracted to the men's table. For one thing, despite my feminist leanings, I have never possessed an innate talent for the sort of conversation required by groups of females—consisting in the main of approvingly smiling and laughing in a high register at things I find so boring I want to individually pull out all the follicles on my face—but mostly because I had a secret, and when you have a secret there is an unfailing attraction to people who are in some way connected to it.

My presence put Harry in fine fettle. There is a kind of man that can only believe that the proximity of a woman is a result of his own magnetism. This put me in good fettle. I had a secret and he didn't know it. The advantage was mine.

He adjusted his performance for my presence. That is to say, whatever he was talking about, doing so louder. I had the advantage and was game. I don't specifically recall what he was talking about, but I provided him with the voice of feminine opposition that put the wind in his sails. Let's say he was rating the relative military prowess of various Indian tribes.

HARRY: The Navajo were good skirmishers, but lacked the focus to become a great warrior nation. Unlike the Sioux, as Colonel Custer could attest. Custer was a prick. Although, Sitting Bull himself could only sleep on his back because he had a wife on either side who hated the other one and wouldn't let him turn the other way, so it just goes to show you.

LEDA: Goes to show you what?

HARRY: But really what we are doing is lubing up before we start talking about the Comanches.

LEDA: Do you ever get tired of the subject of people killing people?

HARRY: People killing people has another name, and that is history, which last time I checked, never hurt anyone to be a student of. So the question as a novelist is whether or not as a man you can write a character tougher than yourself.

LEDA: Who exactly is this question relevant to besides you?

HARRY: It's the central crisis of the male novelist. All fiction is about the test of moral courage, and this ultimately expresses itself in men as physical courage. That's why half the novels worth reading, probably more than half, are novels about war.

LEDA: What you're saying is actually insane. Not insane in the colloquial sense, but like running around in a Napoleon hat and diapers insane.

HARRY: Of course a man can write truthfully about a character of equal or lesser physical courage, but is it possible for him to of write a stronger man without having an ashamed feeling in his stomach that he's lying?

LEDA: Fortunately, woman writers don't have to sit around worrying about something this dumb.

HARRY: I don't know what the equivalent would be for women. Maybe whether or not you can write a character more sensitive than yourself.

LEDA: Oh for the love of God.

HARRY: Those French fries are going right to your ass, by the way.

There were pitchers of beer on the table, but I went inside for something harder. Axioms like "beer before liquor" were the mark of an amateur to me. When I returned Harry pulled me onto his lap.

"You know what I like about you, Oberlin?" he said. His nose was red and his eyes were bleary and filled with that entitlement of proximity. "You're the kind of 'feminist' who doesn't actually have any chick friends."

Austin nights were still warm enough in the fall for there to be a film of sweat on your clothes and the smell of his armpits was strong.

"Wow, does your body actually produce that odor or do you roll around on a dead gorilla before you go out?" I said.

He flexed his biceps, looking pleased.

"Does it make you jealous your boyfriend is taller than you?" I said.

"Aw, the man cub," he said.

Something behind the blear in his eyes became hard and focused as he smiled.

"I just love resting my head on his shoulder at the movies," he said.

I shoved myself off him. Other people were looking over but I was only dimly aware in the tunnel vision of my anger. They had talked about it. Of course they had. What I had believed was to be an understanding, our secret, he had no incentive whatever to hold up. I WAS SUPPOSED TO HAVE A SECRET. He had ruined it, of course he had ruined it. He was just a kid, a twenty-two-year-old kid with this horrible gland of a friend who he had probably told everything to, and I was a silly *LITTLE GIRL* making an idiot of herself, and God knows what snickering, adolescent conversations they had had about me. I felt dizzy. But through my occluded drunk and angry vision I was still aware of the smirk on Harry's face, winning. I vowed never to talk to Jason White again.

truth

L ATER IN OCTOBER THERE was a film festival.
Hogwarts was one of the sponsors, so we
received free badges. This was a blow to
Mark. He had adjusted without complaint to
his status as a plus one. In fact, he had a real
aptitude for it, bestowing the sense that suspending his own
ambitions was a chivalric act. But filmmaking was supposed
to be his world, and a certain luminary of the once-trendy
Mumblecore movement who Mark particularly admired was
premiering his new movie opening night. He didn't say how
unfair this was, neither of us had to. I gently suggested that
he could make a goal of getting a short film in next year's

competition. Wouldn't it be more fun to be there with a film than just getting a free ticket?

"Do you even want me there?" he said.

"Baby, badges are like six hundred dollars."

"It must be nice getting presents for not having to work."

I rubbed his leg.

The opening night film was at the same theater that held the revival series. There was a line wrapped around the building with a group of Hogwarts students toward the middle of it, including Jason and Harry. There was a feeling in my stomach that I decided was annoyance.

For a couple of weeks I'd avoided Jason, and when I did encounter him socially gave him the cold shoulder. I hoped this confused and upset him. He had ruined our secret. I recruited allies to my cause. Being the product of an elite private school education, Shakespeare never invented a character better suited to the task. This Jason person, who I've barely noticed and it's hard to imagine why I'm even talking about him, wouldn't you agree he is abrasive and immature and the worst? Overall, I've been having the most wonderful time, though I have noticed an undercurrent of MALE PRIVILEGE, not to name any names (cough, cough, Jason White)… Getting people to side with you against a loud white idiot in a place like Hogwarts is approximately as difficult as leveling accusations of satanic consort in eighteenth-century Salem.

At my approach Harry made a remark about the weather taking a turn for the Sapphic. Jason did not acknowledge me. This exacerbated my "annoyance."

After the screening there was a migration to the hotel bar, where a large crowd had gathered. Jason continued to ignore me, and I was now in a state of distraction. How immature was he! A few rounds later I found myself giving him a piece of my mind.

"Are you PMS-ing or something?" I said.

He looked at me like I was being the unreasonable one.

I poked him. "*Hi.*"

"So now that you want me to pay attention to you again I'm supposed to pay attention to you again?"

"Um, obviously?"

"I hear you've been saying messed-up stuff about me."

"Are you twelve?"

"I don't think you have to be twelve to object to someone saying messed-up stuff about you."

"I was only doing it so you'd know I was mad at you."

"Why the hell were you mad at me?"

I did not know how to explain, let alone remotely desire to do so. It was good to see him.

"It doesn't matter now because I'm over it."

He considered this. Then he pointed at a decorative saddle and stirrups that was mounted to a post.

"Do you bet me I won't steal that?" he said.

"You can't steal it, there's a million people here."

"What do you bet me I won't steal it?"

"I bet you nothing, because you're not going to, and this is a pointless conversation."

"All right, bet me."

"I would bet you to not be the dumbest person alive but then I would lose."

Harry came over. I masked my impatience at the intrusion—not, I assured myself, that there was anything he was even intruding on.

"I am going to count down from ten and then I am going to punch you in the face," he said to Jason.

"Ten," he said, and punched Jason in the ribs. "You never know when Al-Qaeda will strike."

Jason pointed at the saddle. "Do you bet me I won't steal that?"

"You're the world's most miserable coward if you don't," said Harry.

"Don't call a native-born Texan a coward," said Jason.

"Sorry, I don't speak coward," said Harry.

Jason threw back his drink, and looked around to make sure the bar staff was occupied, then walked over to the saddle and threw the post over his shoulder and ran out the doors with it.

"That dumbass," said Harry. "Now what's he going to do with it?"

The smell of his armpits was somehow more palpable in this crowd, as though even his odor was compelled to dominate the competition. But I was happy; I had the upper hand once more. Harry thought Jason had performed this towering idiocy on his account.

But even if he did not know why, Harry intuited I had the advantage and gave me a considered look. "You know what your whole problem is, Oberlin?"

"Yes, it is waging a full-scale assault on my nostrils as we speak," I said.

"Your problem is that you're a seven who thinks she's a four," he said.

I was too indignant to respond. I didn't know if I was angrier that he was right that I saw myself as a four or that he had only called me a seven.

Moments later Jason came back in and returned the saddle as unobtrusively as possible. He returned to us flushed and chagrined.

"Coward," said Harry.

Later in the night the three of us wound up in the room of the filmmaker being celebrated, in the way of these things that you can't remember exactly how it happened, but can often be attributed to the search for better drugs. There was some pot, but Harry was adamant that someone in this room was holding coke. I hoped not, because Harry was the second to last person I wanted to do coke with; coke is a drug that invites your least favorite person to the party and that person is you. I would still Hoover it if it was ever in front of me, though.

"One of you Communist Hollywood cocksuckers is holding out!" Harry announced in frustration.

No one came forward if this was the case, but it had the unintended effect of fascinating the filmmaker despite no shortage of parasites and toadies, in that feline way that we all feel a subtle pull to the one person in the room who is least interested in impressing us. They were not natural bedfellows: the filmmaker wore loose flannel shirts and an unflattering beard and was overall committed to the indie-film-dude sensibility which, in ordinary circumstances, prompted Harry to make wistful comments about reinstating the draft. He was also the higher status male, which alone could be expected to rouse Harry's ire. But the filmmaker regarded him with such deferential curiosity that any instinctive aversion Harry may have felt was soon overridden by assuming his even more natural role as lecturer. I watched in astonishment as Mark's hero listened credulously to Harry's explanation of the failing of his work.

"The point of narrative is to show the soul in conflict with itself," said Harry. "This is the problem with cocksucking Hollywood."

The filmmaker interjected, politely observing that he worked outside the studio system.

"I don't care about your Hollywood Communist distinctions!" said Harry. "There are basic conflicts of the soul that fuel narrative. Courage, honor, betrayal, fighting the battle in a world of suffering and finding hope. This is life. Unemployed losers who talk like they have a dick in their mouth whose central conflict is deciding what silk screen T-shirt to wear today is not. You have a war going on inside you."

"I think I'm a pretty happy person," said the filmmaker.

"You have a war going on inside you!" said Harry. "And if you are telling stories with anything less than the moral conviction required to win this war, you are actively contributing to the empire's decline."

The filmmaker absorbed this. "Oh man," he said.

I jumped in. "Is it possible for you to have a conversation about art without sounding like Mussolini?"

Harry rolled his eyes toward the filmmaker for support. "This is why woman writers are like woman drivers," he said. "Their emotions are driving the car."

"Fuck you," I said.

He rolled his eyes again.

"*Fuck you*," I said, this time with a quaver in my voice that universally means you are losing ground.

I glared at Jason. He was not the person I was mad at, but I was so mad someone would have to account for it, and Harry had the advantage just then.

I could see that Jason was conflicted. He wanted to come to my defense but it would have meant publically challenging Harry and disrupting their pack equilibrium. I continued glaring at him. This is a moment I look back on with nostalgia. It was the first time I tested him.

"Well, a lot of guys think they're better drivers than they are," said Jason.

"What are you trying to say?" said Harry.

"I'm just saying that most stuff you can say about women you can say the same thing about men, just with more ego."

"Are you trying to tell me you're a Communist?"

"You better not call a native-born Texan a Communist unless you're prepared to reap the consequences."

"As long as the consequence isn't that you sneeze on me so I become a Communist."

"Now you've done it."

Before long they were wrestling, red-faced and wheezing on the floor. It is a natural law that men who start out play-fighting will simply be fighting after thirty seconds and this was no exception. It was soon obvious that Jason was at a disadvantage. Harry was nearly a head shorter, but far stronger, and meaner, and he got Jason into a headlock from which he could not extricate himself with his thrashing knees and elbows.

"Say it," said Harry.

But Jason would not yield. His breath was increasingly ragged as Harry tightened his arm around his windpipe, and Jason flailed more wildly, knocking over a standing lamp.

"Who are these idiots?" said one girl.

The filmmaker hit his joint with a troubled expression. "Do you think my characters lack moral conviction?" he asked me.

I was focused on the display at my feet. Jason's situation was more pathetic by the moment. It looked like he might pass out, but still he pried at Harry's arm, limply, like a tired kitten.

"Let go of him, you gorilla," I said. But…the longer Jason held out, the happier I was.

Harry looked at the room for support. "All he has to do is say it," he said reasonably.

Jason's face was all bunched up now and mottled purple.

"Uncle," he said in a barely audible croak.

Harry released him and Jason flopped to his back and gasped for air.

Harry patted his cheek.

"Look at this face," said Harry.

Jason shoved him away. There was a film of angry and embarrassed tears in Jason's eyes.

"You're a jerk," I said to Harry, and stooped to help Jason up.

But as I did so Harry put a hand to my shoulder, really only fingertips, and stopped me with strange gentleness. He shook his head, also gently, but with authority. I don't know what I found more offensive: the implication that helping Jason up was the incorrect behavior, or the immediate realization that Harry was right.

Jason caught his breath and got to his feet. He put his arm around Harry and said, "Now let that be a lesson to you."

It is customary for members of my sex to express disdain for the idiocy of boys, but I believe this to be a deception born from envy of the luminous simplicity not accorded to women.

Soon we called it a night. Jason and Harry were in the hall, but I stopped to pee and when I came out the filmmaker was obstructing my path to the door. I could see in his face that the affectation of whimsical eccentricity had fallen away, the real thing underneath.

"If you want to stick around, I do have some blow," he said.

I said I was all right.

"Are you seriously going to leave with these clowns?"

"My boyfriend really likes your movies."

"Something tells me you mean that as an insult."

I smiled and brushed past him.

"One time I got a hand job from Amber Heard when she was still a lesbian," he said.

"A hand job isn't much to brag about, even from a lesbian," I said.

He looked at the floor, contrite. "I know."

Downstairs, we got sidetracked at the bar where the last embers of the party still burned, the way that late, liminal hours create a desire for unveiling, to connect with each other more slovenly and vitally. I knew I should go home; the later I was out the more of a slap in the face it was to Mark. I announced I needed to go because I thought being talked out of it would be a fun game. It was. We wound up sitting on the leather couches with a Hogwarts poet from my year who could have cared less about the festival but had been furnished a pass my boyfriend at home couldn't afford and some kid who had been circling her all night. Harry had started circling now and I thought it would probably make for a good show. The girl was close to Jason's age with a kitten diffidence that screamed the type who had been socially and sexually inconsequential in high school but whose Margaret Thatcher glasses and leggings would have made her worshipped by the nerd elite in undergrad (though, between you and me, she did not have the thighs for it). Harry's rival was a wispy, bearded software designer (presumably an alumnus of the nerd elite), though even I could see how ill-matched he was: despite his greater sensitivity and attunement to cultural trends to which Harry was proudly indifferent, the fact was behind the blasé mask she was still more intrigued by the swaggering jock. Before long, Harry had us playing a drinking game of his invention called Truth, which was simply Truth or Dare without the Dare. Its crass elegance and lack of originality yet another reminder of his advertising career—in the number of times I had seen this game played during my Hogwarts career I could think of no more expedient way to get a room full of adults talking explicitly about sex. Of course it was a given we were almost immediately trying to one-up each other with who could come up with the most transgressive questions.

Harry began with the poet, who was the ostensible motivation for starting the game in the first place.

"When was the last time you were spanked by your father?" he said.

She smirked coyly. "It depends who's playing Daddy," she said.

"*Wow*," said the fifth wheel with a nervous laugh. Although I certainly had no interest in how things turned out with the girl apart from schadenfreude out of principle against Harry's sexual success, even I considered this kid a fifth wheel.

"How big is your dick fully erect?" I asked Harry (there was no specific order to gameplay; by Harry's design, whoever was quickest and loudest was the asker).

"*Wow.*" Nervous laughter.

"Six and a half, seven inches."

"It is *not*."

"More than six and a half, less than seven."

"In *inches*."

He shrugged, pleased with himself over how quickly this game was increasing his sexual mystique.

"You have to tell the truth!" I said. "If you don't tell the truth you'll only have daughters and have to self-publish your first novel."

"God's honest truth," he said.

"That's like half your height!"

Even if I had accidentally done him a favor, I could still remind her how short he was.

"And it's actually twice my body weight," he said. "Like a hummingbird."

Jason made a quizzical face.

"You shut your ornithologist mouth!" said Harry. "All right you little ornithologist—have you ever jerked off thinking of someone *in this room*?"

Jason flushed. I was thrilled. *He had to tell the truth.* The cosmology of this game really was reductive somehow, as though simply entering into it vested the rules some metaphysical jurisdiction.

"Yes," he said.

Of course it was as much in Harry's nature to put his closest friend in a deeply uncomfortable spot as it was not in him to allow me to enjoy it for too long.

"What about you, Oberlin?" he said, eyeing me accusingly.

"*Me*? No! Oh my God, no! Oh my God, that question may actually put me *off* masturbation for the rest of my life, so thank you."

The girl looked at me with complacent superiority, like an audience member watching a predictable sitcom plot unfold.

"Oh my God, I *love* your tights," I said. "You have *amazing* legs for tights."

After the game exhausted itself the girl wandered out for a cigarette. Harry and his competitor were at a stalemate: whoever went after her would have been giving the other an advantage in his eagerness, so neither of them followed. Also the kid (evincing some taste, *finally*) started trying to impress me with his screenplay idea that supposedly he and his friends were going to shoot the next year. It was an instantly forgettable premise, equally pretentious and derivative, a zombie satire about a hot new app that shuts down the frontal cortex, but that people were still buying en masse because everybody else had. Harry could not contain an audible groan, as though at a sudden odor.

"What is it with cocksucking zombies?" he said.

"How have you even seen enough movies to have an opinion?" said Jason.

"I read an article in *The New York Review of Books*," said Harry. "But what does it say about the empire that we're afraid of dead people who want to go to the mall? What happened to fucking minotaurs?"

The kid bristled, but tried to sell it as nonchalance.

"Well that's not how the financier sees it," he said.

"Who's financing?" said Jason.

He didn't want to hear about this stupid movie any more than anyone else did but knew that encouraging him would wind Harry up. It was a mildly cruel joke at the kid's expense, but I flattered myself to believe it was to punish him for turning his attention to me.

The "financier," it transpired, was the father of a friend with oil money.

Jason inquired about the budget.

"We're trying to keep it pretty small-scale, like five hundred grand."

He stated this "modest" figure with self-vindication.

Jason continued to ask encouraging questions until Harry rubbed the bridge of his nose wearily and interrupted, "You have five hundred thousand dollars in an escrow account?"

"The money is there," the kid asserted with a curtness implying he didn't know what an escrow account was.

"Look," said Harry, "I consider it an inferior medium— no offense," (this to Jason, who nodded, *none taken*) "but even I know how hard it is to get someone to give you one dollar, let alone a half million of them."

"Well it's a good thing you're not the *financier,*" said the kid, who went on answering Jason's last question about locations.

Harry interrupted again. "Make you a deal. If you keep talking about this, I'm gonna zap you."

The three of us looked at each other in confusion over what this could possibly mean. The kid then resumed talking.

"I'm gonna zap you!" said Harry, happy for the first time this conversation.

"—and I have a friend who can get us a permit for a night shoot at the Capitol building for some real production value."

Harry stood. He took the kid by the shirtfront, pulled him from his chair, and shoved him with explosive force. The kid stumbled back, reeling into the wall. Both Jason and I laughed, in part disbelief that *this* was what "zapping" was and in part because of the instinctive cowardice that makes it more convenient to align against the bullied.

"Nice," said the kid, from an unexpected and shaming reserve of dignity. "I hope you're all very proud of yourselves."

Harry thrust his chest forward as though he was going to charge, and the kid hastily retreated from the bar.

Harry was quiet, his face confused like a chastised dog. He was sensitive enough to know his performance had gone over the line and was trapped between commitment and apology. He shrugged it off, grunting, "Told him," and wandered off, in search of the leggings.

I told Jason to give me a ride home. Idling on the street outside my place I said, "Is that normal for him?"

"For him normal is relative," he said evasively.

"He didn't have to do that," I said. "That wasn't a joke. It was the completely unnecessary humiliation of another person disguised as a joke."

Jason withdrew. The cognitive dissonance that resulted from being confronted with the flaws in his hero worship was a reliable way to push him into Fort Jason.

"And the way he was just so casually dismissive of, you know, the thing you want to do with your life? Do you honestly think it's possible he isn't threatened by how good you are?"

Jason looked out the windshield, quiet. Then he said, "If we can agree I'm not asking you to not hate each other, is there any way you can hate each other but leave me out of it?"

My heart went out to him. His youth was like a tattoo: a thing right in front of you it was easy to forget to see. It really bothered him that his friends couldn't be friends. Up through undergraduate people of diverse temperaments are forced to form a functional ad hoc community, and he had not had enough exposure to the adult world to have discovered the mean truth that sometimes an initial disliking is too much to ever overcome. Freud's "narcissism of minor differences:" the fact that we were more alike than we were different made the contempt that much starker.

I took his hand.

"What's this?" he said, touching the nail of my thumb, which is dented in the middle and discolored.

"My mom shut a door on it. Not maliciously. She was high."

We were quiet. He ran his fingertip along this old injury. We both looked ahead at the fog in the street, waiting for one of us to say something calamitous. There was the sound of Jason's phone getting a text message. I withdrew my hand.

He checked the message, and shook his head with a soundless laugh. I craned my head and he angled the screen so I could see. It was from Harry:

Bitch has a BOYFRIEND. Poets be shoppin'…

I smiled, too, despite myself. Boys being boys… I told Jason I'd see him tomorrow and got out of the truck.

the plight of
the plus one

FOR THE REST OF the weekend Jason and I
attended screenings and events together.
We drank champagne with breakfast and
poured cocktails into my running bottle for
screenings and walked half the city between
venues and also just to walk; every time you step out of a dark
theater and the sun is still out, the world becomes a dazzlingly
pleasant discovery. Like a dog, I came to recognize Jason's
walk: his long stride, the percussion of his boot heels. People

would see us around, and the whispering followed. I didn't care. At Hogwarts, like any environment where everyone knows everyone else's name, gossip is the currency of choice, especially after I had so recently been his vocal detractor. But they didn't understand, I told myself, without going so far as identifying the source of their confusion.

Then on Monday, the whiplash. I could not get back to work despite having lost the weekend, and when I tried to read my eyes slid off the page. Returning so abruptly to my routine was like getting the bends, like my bones telling me everything was wrong. Mark asked if I was okay. He transitioned seamlessly from being jealous of my privilege to expressing sympathy for my being unaccountably upset over it. This only contributed to my feeling of overwhelming and immutable wrongness. I said I was just tired. I wanted to tell him, *Your idol tried to fuck me and when's the last time you did.*

The next week we hosted a small dinner party at Mark's suggestion. Initially I vetoed this plan; it had been years since I'd had an independent social identity and had almost physical aversion to presenting a united domestic front when I could be out at bars. I told him there was something a *little* patriarchal about him volunteering me to play wifey-poo; we both knew realistically all organization would fall to me. I could not have cared less about this argument—cooking

for friends is an activity I have always found enjoyable—
but being my mother's daughter I reflexively maximize the
leverage of a given situation, and *I really really really don't feel
like it* will always be trumped by obscure fault on the other
party's end.

Mark apologized and sulked. At first I was surprised by
the extent of his disappointment, but then it was obvious that
his desire for it to happen had the same root as my desire
against: he wanted to be part of a life that was including him
less and less.

I relented, and the dinner was most glaring as a model
of civilized behavior, even from Jason and Harry. As is the
norm in literate circles, Harry's first stop was my bookshelf,
and, upon evaluation, gave it an approving nod that I did
not interpret as veiled judgment or sabotage. To prevent the
conversation from getting too Inside Baseball with Hogwarts
gossip, Jason began discussing with Mark the various merits
of the Red Camera versus the Alexa with Harry nodding
along as though he didn't consider the ephemera of film
technology brain-meltingly boring; Mark progressively
warmed up through the wine and feeling like part of the
group and Harry indulged him with flattery. He began a
discourse on the plight of the plus one, the strain it put on
relationships. I had to remind myself to stop pouring wine in
my glass after it was over two-thirds full.

"When my wife went back to school I was a plus one, and it takes a lot of strength of character to support someone through that," said Harry.

"You were married?" said Mark.

"Yeah. Then she fucked one of her professors in the coatroom of a party. But she was a no-good treacherous whore who will rue the day she did that to the next great American novelist."

"Oh, *man*," said Mark.

"Anyway, you found yourself a good one," Harry informed me.

"Well, she's the lightning, I'm the bottle," said Mark.

I smiled and discreetly pressed my fork into the flesh of my thigh under the table hard enough to leave marks.

wings

ONE DAY IN NOVEMBER Jason and I had plans to see a movie that was high on our anticipation list, a fall awards-bait kind of thing that had garnered advance notoriety because of some kinky sex scenes that had caused it to be initially rated NC-17. We still saw movies together regularly, preferably just the two of us, other times in groups where it became impossible for me to focus on what was on-screen if we were not sitting next to each other. On one occasion, we went to three in a single day; there was by now a compulsive quality to the way we saw *everything*, this vicarious rush of *kiss kiss bang bang* sublimating the increasingly incautious truth neither of us spoke, this unspoken thing drying my mouth so that sitting next to him in the dark sometimes it felt like swallowing was ten thousand decibels. So it was a rude shock the day this particular quasi-dirty movie opened he sent me a perfunctory text saying he couldn't make it with no further explanation.

I took a moment to present myself as less frantic than I was and called him. He didn't pick up. *What?!* Clearly he had his phone with him, he had only just texted me. I nearly called him again but decided this would definitely come off as desperate and refused to give him the satisfaction. What satisfaction? Was I really so narcissistic to believe my emotional reaction to this rain check was even relevant in the face of whatever had motivated it? And *was* it a rain check, or an outright cancellation? It was all so infuriatingly cryptic, but reason prevailed that calling again would be fruitless regardless of losing face because he could clearly see that I had called, and was owed an explanation—this phrase *OWED AN EXPLANATION* throbbing in my thumb as it redialed.

Once more he didn't answer. I was in a state. On the one hand there was the indignation he had just ignored two of my calls, but on the other supposing there was a perfectly valid explanation—or even if there wasn't—the amount of face I had certainly lost from the second call. But now there was nothing to do but wait, and maintain as dignified and casual a façade as possible until he contacted me. Waiting was the only option. Unless...

I decided to send him a self-effacing text message communicating how not a big deal it was to dispel the illusion of being a basket case on my end, in the event he was simply not in a position to make a call but believed one was due because I myself had called twice, thus giving him the opportunity to simply text in response the explanation I WAS OWED. I composed such a casually self-effacing message, including a highly specific inside joke between us, revised it several times to my satisfaction—including the addition of a typo to make it appear more dashed off—and sent it.

A few minutes passed with no reply. I was in a STATE. Unless his phone had died in the interim there was no reason I could imagine that would prevent him from taking a couple of seconds to reply to my clearly dashed-off *ha ha* message communicating that it was NO BIG DEAL he was flaking on our movie date—not that "date" was the right word—but how about some MANNERS. Then a thought crippled me: he may not have actually *gotten* the inside joke on which the comedic inflection of my message hinged, compelling me to send an even more self-effacing follow-up clarifying the tone of the first one. I felt like I was cutting my own hair and making it worse but with every attempted correction, unable to abandon the pathology it was salvageable.

But srsly: NBD!! I sent.

An hour later I broke down and called Harry. There was suspicion in his voice. We were certainly not chatting on the phone with any regularity, but I spent a few minutes pretending to solicit his input on classes for the next term on the assumption that listening to himself give advice would lower his guard before ever so casually asking if he had spoken to Jason that day.

"The man cub?" he said, the suspicious tone instantly returning. "Not recently. Why?"

"No reason," I said.

There was silence on the line.

"We were supposed to hang out today," I blurted, at least refraining from specifying our movie date (not a date!), "but he bailed under, like, mysterious circumstances, and I just wanted to make sure nothing was up."

"I haven't talked to him," said Harry.

"Not that it's a big deal," I said. "It's not a big deal at all, I just thought I'd, you know, check in."

"…Okay," said Harry.

"Anyway, I'll let you get back to having a tea party with your guns, or whatever it is you do with your time."

"… Okay," said Harry.

There was silence on the line.

"Is he mad at me?" I blurted.

"Why would he be mad at you?"

"I don't know, he got mad at me before."

"He got mad at you because you got mad at him."

"Well I'm not mad at him!"

There was another silence.

"I haven't reached eight hundred words yet today," he said.

"Fine, fine, fine!" I said. "This is totally *fine*."

I hung up, in a shame spiral over the actual reason I was hemorrhaging so much dignity: the crashing disappointment I wasn't going to get to sit next to Jason and watch perv-y sex scenes, as I had been looking forward to for weeks.

At this point, more as an act of masochism than a genuine attempt at communication, I texted Jason: *Are you mad at me?*

His reply was nearly immediate: *? Just swamped. Lemme know how the movie is*

I swung from self-pity back into irate exegesis:

?—as though there was not yet another stupidly maddening mystery contained within the speed of his reply, implying he'd had his phone on him THE ENTIRE TIME and was intentionally not responding.

Just swamped—with WHAT, exactly? I knew he worked as regularly as a metronome in the mornings, imitating Harry's imitation of Hemingway, intentionally filling his schedule with Mickey Mouse classes as well as writing comments on classmates' stuff during workshop itself to keep his non-writing schedule as idle as possible. It was a recurring joke within our Hogwarts circle being that he was the world's youngest retiree. So this was not only a lie but a lie that *he knew I knew* was a lie, as opposed to, say, CAR TROUBLE or TOOTHACHE or any of the endless polite excuses if he was not subtly insinuating this was a blow-off.

"Lemme know how the movie is"—confirming this was *not* a rain check; he was just as happy to see OUR movie in his own time with someone else and would probably use the smutty stuff as way to start pontificating on the eroticism of transgression or whatever intellectual peacocking to get a nineteen-year-old communications major let him feel her up.

I commanded myself to think about other things, but for the entire weekend thought of little else, turning around the dozen or so words from this message with rabbinical fervor.

✦

MARK AND I WENT to the movie ourselves. It turned out to be a boringly unhot disappointment and I was an incorrigible bitch to him all night.

✦

ON MONDAY AFTER CLASS I saw a letter in my school mail slot. The envelope was unmarked except with an *L*. My heart raced irrationally; my brain attempted to calm it like an unruly pet. I stepped out the back way to avoid the smokers' circle in front and removed the letter. It was a single line:

I'm in love with you, for the record. J

I folded the letter back into thirds, put it back into the envelope, and joined my classmates for the customary lunch, politely dismissing comments about my distraction and lack of appetite. At home I placed the letter in the middle of a Norton anthology I could not imagine Mark opening but thought better of it, then slipped it in my files among previous years' tax returns, but again *what if* troubled me, so finally I took a small ball of sticky tack and fixed it to the inner wall of a crawlspace full of cleaning supplies.

The front door opened unexpectedly and I grabbed a bottle of window cleaner and closed the door of the crawl space.

"Hey," said Mark. "Client canceled last minute. I can make myself scarce if you're working."

"Oh no," I said. "It's okay."

"What? Why are you smiling?"

"I'm just having a really nice day."

✦

"It's impossible," I said.

Jason smiled with defensive impatience.

"I didn't need you to tell me that," he said.

It was afternoon and we were sitting in a booth at a circus-themed dive bar adjacent to the city's less affluent mall. It was a sufficiently random meeting place that the chance of being interrupted by anyone we knew was minimal, and the run-down fiberglass animal gothic was gaudily, tragically romantic.

"This was a really good choice, *incidentally*," I said. "You have very cinematic instincts for curating moments."

Jason shrugged with self-satisfaction, the vanity of artists susceptible in any situation.

"You're still crazy," I said. "You're *crazy*, you know that? You're twelve years old, you have very shapely effeminate lips,

I'm *flattered*—don't get me wrong, this temporary insanity is *highly* flattering—but it's impossible."

"What if we take for granted that I'm not the kind of guy who tries to bird-dog someone else's girl, and that I wouldn't even have told you in the first place except I had had a realization, and it was that I have lost almost all interest in having a conversation with anyone who isn't you? Which is deeply annoying because I really, really like talking."

There was a joyful sensation in my stomach that wanted nothing more than to tell him I felt exactly the same way.

I shook my head and said, "Silly boy."

He looked capable of murder and I could hardly have held it against him.

"Don't play it that way," he said, making eye contact with the almost scary firmness he was capable of at times, and which was highly becoming on him.

"Okay, simmer down," I said.

I poured bourbon into my glass. This was the kind of bar that didn't have a liquor license so you could bring your own and they would furnish the set up. I regarded the Diet Coke in my hand.

"Ugh, aspartame," I said. "My mother always said everything either gives you cancer or makes you fat. But being fat makes you more likely to get cancer, so."

I added Diet Coke to the drink.

"I don't mean to trivialize what you're telling me," I said. "If it seems like I am, it's a nervous reaction to what you're saying."

"I know," he said.

"Assumed! I assume when you look at people you don't see flesh and blood, you see a sort of cloud of ones and zeros in a humanoid shape. No one is questioning your cleverness— though your *judgment* is a different story."

"Meaning what."

"You're *crazy*. I'm old enough to be your *mother*, practically, and I'm pretty much married."

"You're three and a half years older than me."

"Which is decades in girl years."

"And when in the history of romantic love has unavailability been a deterrent?"

"You don't even know what love is! Love is not letting go. It's not letting go just because things are different than they used to be, they're not as exciting as they used to be, they can never be exciting as something new that comes along. But you remember the good things, you look for the good things with a *microscope*, and you don't throw away all the years you've spent…refusing to let this fail."

"I think that's a narrow definition."

"Who asked you?" I said, with an intended flippancy that came out caustic.

"I didn't mean that in a judgy way," he said.

"I know you didn't." I exhaled. "You're quite sweet, actually. I just get moody sometimes. You should know I'm no prize. I'm unpredictably moody and I'm short without being petite *or* having big tits and you'd be sick of me so much faster than you realize."

"Just to clarify," said Jason, "the reason this is an impossible situation is Mark, and not because it's one-sided."

"If the question is if I happened to have a younger sister would my heart burst like a Jewish grandmother's over the match, then yes, it would burst like a Jewish grandmother's. If the question is if we would ever sleep together in a thousand years, I'm sorry, I just don't feel that way about you."

"I'm trying to decide if setting me up with your imaginary younger sister is more or less insulting than if you'd said you think of me like a brother."

"I assume you have perverted ideas about the eroticism of transgression and I'm not sure saying you were like a brother would convey how asexual my feelings for you are."

He regarded the carousel behind the bar. Then he said, "Did you throw it away?"

I pretended I didn't know what he was talking about.

"Did you throw away the note?" he persisted.

"No, I didn't throw it away."

"Why didn't you throw it away?"

"Because what I do with my mail is my business."

"Why wouldn't you throw it away when Mark might find it?"

"How do you know I didn't show it to Mark already?"

"Because you didn't."

"It's none of your business either way."

"Throw it away."

"No."

"Throw away the note."

"It's mine, you don't get to tell me what to do with it."

"Give it to me. I'll rip it up and throw it away myself."

"No."

I let my head lull backward with an exasperated groan.

"I'm a woman, Jason. I'm not the world's most desirable woman, but even I know how easy it is to confuse flattery with opportunity. But I respect you too much to lead you on, and I will never sleep with you."

"You do realize the more times you say that the less likely it is to be true."

I looked down at the table, trying to hide my pleased smirk.

"Do you know what a satellite male is?" he said.

I didn't.

"In biological terms a satellite male is the guy who orbits the prospective female until she lets her guard down long enough for him to mate. Of course it is customary for a female with market value to have any number of satellite male friends who make a big thing of how sensitive and understanding they are but are actually waiting for the slightest moment of vulnerability to make impact. If this is what you want, by all means find yourself a Europa who will go shopping with you and listen to your relationship problems and every once in awhile if you're feeling drunk or daring you might cuddle with. But that won't be me."

"That's so romantic you think I'm 'a female with market value,'" I said.

He said nothing.

"It really changes now, doesn't it?" I said. "It's not going to be able to go back to how it was before."

"You mean you're not going to be able to keep having your cake and eating it, too?"

My stomach was in knots, suddenly. It was grief, my unreadiness for this friendship to end and the knowledge that this wasn't the sort of thing a friendship survived, not really. I didn't want to lose him, even less than I wanted to admit the impossibility of holding onto a deception once it has been named, once he has opened his stupid mouth and called it by its name.

"Is that too much to ask?" I said.

✦

It did ruin things after that. Following our conversation at the bar I convinced myself that the visceral sense something was over had been false, and all I had to do was give him a few days to get over it. But when I messaged him a few days later to hang out in some innocuous context he responded simply with: *I am not a Europa.*

Angry that he was not over it already, I replied: *No u r URANUS.*

There was nothing more from his end, and when I realized nothing was forthcoming it felt like no amount of inhalation could provide enough oxygen. One of my first visits that semester had been to Student Health for a Xanax prescription, but because of the meagerness of the university insurance had been sheepishly advised by the counselor in the event of an anxiety attack to run, run just as fast as I can until it went away. I stared at the counselor, wondering if she had ever encountered another actual person in her life. My phone lay on my writing desk blackly and silently sucking all the oxygen from the room and I childishly flicked it away as I was overtaken with convulsive sobs. It was the opposite of the feeling of exorbitant potential I had been swept by in the first stage of my friendship with Jason. I could not understand how you could go from that to this feeling of everything being so impossible.

For his part, Jason began snubbing me at group outings. Not actually snubbing, the weapon he used against me was far worse: civility. He was *civil* with me but gave me no special attention, and conversed with others as though it was all the same as talking to *me*. At a reception for a visiting writer, he spent altogether too long in conversation with the most boringly nice Connecticut divorce fiction writer at Hogwarts, someone my own threshold for was under ten minutes and I was substantially more tolerant of boring niceness than Jason, who was talking one-on-one with her at length about the frustrations of putting together Ikea furniture for no other reason than to spite me eavesdropping on it. When it became too much I went over and threaded my arm through his and "borrowed" him.

"I am amused, *if* you're wondering," I said. "I do find it highly *amusing.*"

"I don't know what you're talking about."

"There are less childish ways to go about this, you know," I said. "There is a way to handle this like reasonable adults."

"Is there a reasonable adult way to inform someone they're being fucking crazy?"

"I'm crazy. Oh, *I'm* being crazy. Well, it's part of why you're so fond of me."

"I'm not fond of you, I'm in love with you."

"*Lower* your voice."

"*You* started the conversation."

"Because you're being *unreasonable*."

"What exactly do you want from me?"

"Simmer down," I said. "I want to go to a movie with you. What's opening this week?"

"We don't go to movies anymore."

"Why not."

"Because I'm *in love with you.*"

I hit him. "*Shh*! Why don't you put in the newsletter?"

His eyes flared and he was about to reply when we were approached by a mutual friend who did not realize this was a private conversation.

I took the newcomer's arm and indicated a Borges collection on the shelf.

"Settle an argument. Is it Bor-*hayz* or Bor-*heez*? He is in an absolute *lather* about it."

I indicated Jason, his face a shell so brittle it seemed like you could crack it with the round end of a spoon. I bit the tip of my tongue to prevent myself from laughing with pleasure, knowing the sight of a person preventing themselves from laughing was so much worse.

So it went: Jason torturing me with civility and me torturing him with being a little bitch. Maybe that seems unfair on my end, but in case there is any doubt let's be clear that Jason, even at that age, was one of the most manipulative people I'd ever met. He never didn't know what he was doing. He was aware what a shock standing me up would be, followed by the confession, and then the friend-dumping all in succession. He was aware that saying he wouldn't chase another man's girl was nonsense—his sense of Darwinian entitlement was far too great—but that it romanticized him and offended my ego: what was *stopping* him? And he certainly knew the power of indifference: had he started being actively shitty to me after the friend-dumping I could have tolerated it, but civility I could not.

I texted him drunkenly: *I think u r actually a fucking sociopath.*

He replied: *I miss you, too.*

At this point in the exercise it can fairly be asked what was going on in my head at the time. Or what I thought was going on. Looking at the person I was then, at the meteoric inanity of my own behavior, here is what I have to say about it: men will have you believe they have the market cornered on compartmentalization, but this is not the truth. Say that my brain at the time was a house with many rooms, and that I found myself in the room with the truth in it, but what I *wanted* was in the next room. I went to the next room. I possessed the liar's greatest power, which was to believe her own lies. It is a feast of crows to admit this, confirming Harry's cosmology, but now I don't tell lies anymore just as I don't drink, as relentless as both make facing the day.

I am from Pittsburgh. We have a way of doing things. This does not entail moving our stable and loyal and predictable man to an emotionally unruly place and risking this, that single and infinitely slackened cord connecting our feet to the ground, for a long and tall twenty-two-year-old borderline-autistic Texan with dreams of Hollywood who would leave us for some awful and terrifying nymphet with whom he would share a sad shake of the head over that poor what-was-her-name from grad school who had been pitiable enough to fall in love with him. I wanted to press a hot iron into their faces, and to see him again as soon as possible.

One night during this period, I saw Jason in a dream. Well, not a dream exactly; I had just woken from my normal dreams of trying to escape from some unseen malevolence, and in a semi-lucid state Jason appeared to me, and there was something distinct about this unwelcome apparition: he had wings. But there was something odder still about them—they were not fully feathered wings, but more like the glowing outline of them, as though formed out of neon tubing, and they were crippled, stunted, far too small for his size, and all twisted up, like they had been broken and healed wrong. My heart expanded at the same rate its cage contracted and I was forced to admit it to myself. There was no next room. My love for him was a skyscraper from which I wanted to hurl him off the highest floor.

The next morning I prepared by writing the words I would never speak out loud (*I love Jason White*) and took a walk, tearing up the page and dropped every piece of it in a different trash can. After that I got a steak. It had been years since I'd eaten meat, but had made one last ditch attempt to convince myself that I wasn't feeling what I was feeling, I was just anemic. Then I lay on the floor of my apartment listening to obnoxiously angst-ridden music from my adolescence as my stomach was turning on the meat and also the way your whole body will turn on you no matter how old you are when you're thinking of some boy.

interlude: changeling

I T IS AT THIS point that this epistle must make an unforgiveable turn for the Dickensian, as the author is forced to excavate her origins, due to their impending intrusion on the narrative:

The girl spent her entire childhood awaiting her mother's imminent death. This was because Diane Galvan was regularly predicting it. She was chronically afflicted with a series of ailments, falling into three categories. The first was real, and consisted mainly of neck and spinal problems from

*the physical contortions required of her regular return to the
local gentleman's club main stage when other employment
opportunities didn't pan out. She loved lording this over the
girl, that she was literally KILLING HERSELF to put food
on their table. But the girl saw past this early on, wondering
what nobler instinct exactly was preventing her mother from
maintaining a menial job at Applebee's or GNC, much less
why her departure from these jobs so frequently involved her
threatening frivolous litigation or a more dignified extended
middle finger. Not that the girl ever voiced this; what Diane
needed more than anything—and no small factor in her fifteen
years on and off the pole—was a stage, and there was no better
audience than her daughter, whose suspension of disbelief
allowed her to be moved by every performance.*

*The second category was psychosomatic: most often
phantom and undiagnosable nerve pain leading her to postulate
the most outlandish conspiracies on the part of the medical
community, but sometimes more creative, like the conviction
she was losing her sight (confessed with a tearful,* "I'm just sorry
I won't be able to see my beautiful daughter anymore"), *or
African Sleeping Sickness. This last one even the girl lacking the
vocabulary for it recognized as clinical depression, and believed
to be curable through her own arbitrary magical intervention*
("If I can hold my breath under water in the bathtub for this
many seconds…" "If I can hop down the stairs on one foot

without touching the banister...") *and thus her fault that she failed to make her mother happier.*

The third category was pure fantasy: diseases which there was no particular reason to anticipate, but which Diane would point out, with some wistfulness, could strike her at any moment given her run. Cancer was the natural go-to—"Even thinking the word 'cancer' makes you more likely to get it," *Diane would assert. Other favorites were STDs transmittable through unhygienic public restrooms* ("People are animals, Lee"), *multiple sclerosis* ("Mummy's bones could be turning into a wet fart right in front of you and you would never know"), *or pretty much whatever the disease of the week happened to be on a given hospital procedural.*

Although the girl had her doubts about the intolerable offenses that kept her mother from maintaining a job with all her clothes on, intrinsic narcissistic superstition made her take the hypochondria more seriously. Suppose the fact of her doubt was what caused this affliction to be the mortal one? It was said she was born with one foot in this world and one in the next. It was not impossible. Once when she was six or seven, she had a dream that her mother had cracked like an egg and that the girl cradled her helplessly as viscous stuff drained from the crack. Upon waking from this dream the girl crawled into her mother's bed—Diane was not home from work, but it smelled like her—and shook and shook. She tried imagining what her life would be like without her mother, but it was like imagining the sun falling from the sky, there was no such thing as life after that. She did, however, imagine grown-ups at the funeral whispering to each other how pretty she looked in her grieving (as with her fantasy of entering a convent, a common theme of her young imaginary life was the observation of her prettiness within a context of some highly ritualized grieving).

✦

DIANE GALVAN: TEXTBOOK WHITE trash drama queen, though no queen was more contemptuous to waiters or cab drivers or anyone in a position of servitude. She cackled at the misfortunes of others as though at the plot turns of a potboiler— divorce, miscarriage, bankruptcy, death, any currency of suffering would suffice—while making opulent displays of public sympathy, believing herself to be indispensable to the healing process, that her indispensability was something noticed and discussed with equal importance as the tragic event which had befallen. For her, gift giving was a supreme opportunity for veiled insult: aerobics videos, a guide to dating success, Neutrogena anti-wrinkle cream. There was no story she couldn't top, whether from her own repertoire or whatever her grandiosity decided was true in the moment, no gossip too malicious to repeat (or invent), no incident she couldn't relate back to the materia prima (herself), no dispute she couldn't manipulate to her advantage by deploying her flying monkeys of obfuscation, rage, and pity. There was no display too brazen as long as there was an audience, no audience more captive than her own child.

Where was the father in all this? Of course, keeping his distance. John Kelly possessed a Mensa-level IQ and Thoreau-level ambition—which is to say his justification for his lack of ambition was having read Thoreau in graduate school. He taught psychology at a local community college, where the relaxed competition for tenure, and, more relevantly, convenient campus parking, were more congenial to his disposition. In truth, he was cursed with a demon named DISTRACTION. He could complete the Cryptoquip without the use of a pen and his at-home Jeopardy score was nearly always higher than the episode's winner, but something always came along to distract him from this article or that book idea or whatever application of his potential might elevate his station in life. The great DISTRACTION of his life was Diane Galvan. Combining Eve's milky flesh with the heart of the serpent, if Diane appeared in a private eye's office, face streaked with mascara tears, you could safely turn off the movie right there—did you really need to see how this ended? She had recently returned from Hollywood (the Valley) where her acting career had failed to take off, and had enrolled in his community extension course under the belief this would deepen her understanding of her craft. No Galvan had ever completed college, and she held his role as educator in almost mystical esteem. She liked his talent for words and dark wit, the promise it contained of more expansive realms of darkness over which she could gain sovereignty. He was also already married, which sealed the deal.

John Kelly, for his part, was going through one of his regular periods of despair, in the grand tradition of analytical Irishman congenitally incapable of applying his skillset to making himself happy. He was spending more time at the bar and less with his wife who was barely hiding her resentment at his inability to conceive. He thought Diane was a sorceress. She made him feel like a man again, which is to say she made him feel like a boy again, which is to say she made him hard again. She asked him why a powerful man had married such a MEDIOCRE woman.

Before long both mistress and wife were pregnant, and reaping the consequences of this potency boom, John responded in time-honored fashion by calling his mistress a whore and denying paternity of her unborn child.

✦

Thus denied her previous revenue stream or any financial support, Diane found herself evicted from her apartment and living out of her car when one night, a summer night when the barometric pressure was low and the air sweet with a storm that never arrived, Diane woke and saw a mysterious shimmering in the sky. Curious, she got out. The shimmering descended in a parabola in her direction, and as it did, resolved into clear shapes: orbs of pale blue light. These lights, baseball-size more or less, sought her out with intentional grace and orbited her pregnant stomach several times. There was no sound she could hear but the hairs of her arms detected a vibratory hum that she knew was the singing of the lights, the lights singing to her womb. Then they re-formed into a line and ascended back to the mysterious sphere where they belonged.

Meanwhile John, hearing the news of Diane's straits, did come around with support—while maintaining public skepticism about parentage—and the child ultimately came into this world in a comfortable hospital birth. (At the same time his wife miscarried—a development he never shook the obscure conviction that Diane had willed into reality.) When delivered into Diane's arms, the child looked straight into her eyes with an intelligence beyond years, beyond humanity, and spoke in what was no recognizable language but with the obvious syntax and coherence of an alien tongue. It was then Diane knew the girl had been replaced with a changeling, a strange visitor from the land of the lights, though this changeling never again spoke in its native language and it remains a mystery to this day what message she delivered.

✦

If nothing else, one *thing could be said of being a child of Diane's: it was never boring. Whether her mother was beseeching the girl's absolution that mummy was not a bad person for the latest marriage she was wrecking; or going on vitriolic diatribes against the snobs who shopped at the Ross Park Mall while investing in the latest shortcut to Internet millions or vaguely malevolent self-actualization workshop that wouldn't let you to get up to pee in order to SHOW THEM WHAT WE'RE MADE OF (the factioning of mother-daughter versus the rest of the world was a consistent theme); or hemming the plaid dress of her school uniform while the other girls had to fold them over at the waist to make them more revealing; or decadent hooky days spent shopping at Plato's Closet and eating Pittsburgh-style "salads" consisting of wilted romaine lettuce under mounds of French fries and melted cheese, then renting a stack of movies from the Giant Eagle and reenacting favored scenes from* Mommy Dearest, Grey Gardens, *and* All About Eve; *or being overtaken by one of her dark spells and verbally attacking her daughter with the viciousness of a cat whose affections had reversed, with the viciousness reserved for attacking a part of yourself (it was to come as some surprise in the girl's late childhood to learn that the word "cunt" was considered problematic); or looking at her daughter through eyes intoxicated by love and benzos and marvel at where this beautiful spirit, the only light of her life, the only good thing she ever did, could have come from. The girl derived two operative lessons from a mother singularly unsuited for the task. One was survival. Diane's erratic work schedule and personal affairs forced the girl to adopt a latchkey self-sufficiency, in addition to a high level of adaptability to wildly shifting emotional terrain (her academic excellence a product of both her mother's class anxiety and the relief of a structure in which the laws of cause and effect were so clearly delineated). The other was that there is no more seductive feeling in the world than to be needed.*

When she was fourteen, Diane visited the girl at the prestigious preparatory school she was attending on scholarship (a result of her own aptitude and Diane's goading). But despite this achievement having been no small part of Diane's scheme that this was infiltration from the inside, to SHOW THEM WHAT WE'RE MADE OF, this visit gave Diane no happiness and her discomfort with the environment manifested as an exaggerated provincialism: dialing up her Pittsburgh accent, the same accent the girl was giving herself nightly elocution lessons to neutralize; wandering the campus in a doddering shuffle the girl had to command her own legs to keep pace with, because of their own accord they wanted to keep just enough steps ahead they might not be mistaken for the same party; stopping in the open to fish a joint from her purse and take hits with a strained larcenous grin as though she were being riotously entertaining and not as embarrassing as the grin's flicker suggested she knew was the truth. Previously, Diane's figure had been her pride—in the dressing room of the club she would flick the rear ends of the girls whose lifestyles were catching up with them saying, What's that? What's that? *—but by now her looks had gone and her hips had spread, whereas the girl was not far from attaining what were to be her adult measurements. Similarly, her heart attained mature new proportions when a handsome lacrosse player with whom she was to end up drunkenly fumbling before the semester's end came up to say hello, and Diane's voice went higher in register and her laugh became a coo and she all but put a strand of her own hair into her mouth. The girl had not known it was possible to feel so much superiority and pity at the same time. After a separation of only weeks, her disbelief had finally suspended, seeing her mother in a new light: weak. Upon her departure Diane hugged her daughter and said,* I always knew Mummy wasn't the only actress in the family. *Shortly after that the health of the girl's philodendron took a sharp* *turn for the worse. Suspicious, she sniffed the basin of the pot, which was dank and sour with the smell of vodka. Years later Diane nearly compelled the girl to miss her own graduation ceremony: she writhed around on the floor of her hotel room moaning with sudden incapacitating back pain. It was only when John Kelly intervened and called her bluff, offering to stay with her instead, that she believed with a little oxy she could bring herself to make yet one more sacrifice for the sake of her beautiful daughter, the only light in her life, the only good thing she ever did.*

✦

*D*URING THAT PERIOD, HER *mother married a man named George who had been an on-again, off-again presence throughout the girl's adolescence. George was grossly overweight and bald, with glasses and a mustache that made him look like the stereotype of a pizza maker, and in fact he managed a chain pizza restaurant. He was a passive, angry man whose few enthusiasms included ham radio and right-wing conspiracies. Diane was continually accusing him of cheating on her with the little whores at his restaurant and once assaulted him with a pair of scissors, cutting off a tuft of the hair from the side of his head with the grin of having collected a scalp. George's nose* *would go mottled red and from time to time he would break things, but overall was little fazed by her outbursts. Despite the famed assertion that all unhappy families are unhappy in their own way, in the blue collar Italian-American community, there is an accepted Kabuki of dysfunction. The girl was bemused by her mother's accusations, because Diane herself was still fucking her black drug dealer (which, given George's enlightened views on race and criminality, would cause Diane to say dreamily,* I just don't know what he'd do if he found out...*), not to mention the sheer credit it was giving George initiative-wise.*

But her stepfather surprised her when she was visiting home over Christmas break her sophomore year of undergraduate. She was asleep in her room one morning when she felt another body enter the bed. Stirred half-awake she smiled, believing this body to be Mark, with whom she was now involved. But Mark was with his own family, and she realized this incongruity at the same time she recognized the heavy rolling nose breathing. Adrenaline jolted her awake as he put his arm around her in a spoon, and after a tentative pause began grinding his pelvis into her. She was at a loss. She had gone to a prep school with privileged young monsters, she knew what rape felt like, and this was not that. There had been a pause between his entering the bed and putting his arm around her, and another before he started grinding. He was testing the waters, interpreting her nonresistance as consent. Her indecision was half bafflement: though no stranger to the vagaries of her mother's relationship with reality, she had discounted the marvelous complexity of a brain belonging to a primitive this banal that could convince itself the girl was into this. Even a person so much less interesting than you contains mysteries.

Thankfully a less philosophical sector of her brain stepped in and she heard herself bleat stupidly I have to go to the bathroom, *and with jerky haste she propelled herself from the bed and out of the room.*

For a few days she pretended nothing had happened, a pretense George was more than happy to collude with, but ultimately the girl wound up drunkenly confiding in a cousin. Of course no Galvan can tolerate a secret dampening a good fireworks display, so shortly enough Diane was informed. George, cornered, did not deny the charge. Instead he claimed he had been tired and gotten mixed up and thought the girl was Diane. This was by any measure insane. Out of necessity Diane was maintaining a job as receptionist at dentist's office that required her to leave early in the morning, and it was the wrong room, and at this point confusing Diane for her daughter would have been like confusing Laurel for Hardy. The insanity was the point. Had he denied it, rational doubt could have gained purchase, instead this flimsy pretext—the flimsiest perhaps in all of human history—gave Diane's own insanity something to work with. The relief that the sexual power that had once been her defining quality had not been usurped by the competition: youth, the traitorous nature of flesh. For good measure, she kicked the girl out of the house.

✦

THERE OUGHT TO BE a word for the reverse of namaste: the darkness in me acknowledges the darkness in you. In this context, "acknowledge" would be interchangeable with "must destroy." Power corrupts, and no power supersedes maternity; the universe is so unreasonably respectful of freedom that it has never once forced a person to change against her will. The wheel once again turned, George was gone from the picture and Diane was jobless, and deep in medical debt. Invoking the spirit of the mother-daughter team with backs against the wall to a hostile world, she proposed refinancing her mortgage in the girl's name. The girl and Mark had recently moved to New York; even in their modest Harlem apartment it was not uncommon for her to wake up with her heart racing over financial anxiety. From her father she had learned the term "malignant narcissist," and, from several years of her own alcoholism and an enabling boyfriend who loved her and her own whimsical cruelties with a child's credulity, she had learned that like any unthinking animal, a Galvan will act exactly to the limits of its leash. A lifetime of emotional vampirism was one thing— there is a luxurious reciprocity to all parasitic relationships, the sense of unsurpassable importance as you are being consumed—but this was something else. The girl believed she had a destiny, a quality inherited and refined by her mother's grandiosity. At the same time, she was an adapter, a survivor, trained from childhood. No one was going to get between her and her future, not even the mother whose dependency was as addictive as an infant's. As she formulated her refusal, she was approached by Mark, his face messenger-grim. He had been searching for an aspirin, but Diane kept all pharmaceuticals in her room—out of both convenience and mistrust of which houseguests might help themselves to her medicine cabinet. Going through her drawers he'd found the girl's driver's license, which she had believed she'd misplaced at a bar. The girl went numb. She did not know what the scheme was—her mother could not be bothered to park her car on a different street to throw off relocation agents, let alone successfully perform an act of identity theft. But regardless of her specific intention, what could be assumed was its self-justification, that Diane's martyrdom would have convinced her she was only taking her due because of her ungrateful daughter's unwillingness to SAVE HER FROM THE STREETS, or whatever tear-soaked soliloquy she delivered from the proscenium of her own crazy.

The girl was left with no choice; she was suffused with a pitiless grace, something greater than and originating from outside herself. (This was her first notable experience of the Higher Power around which the benevolent cult, of which she is currently a member, is constructed.) She was a person with a destiny. But the paradox of destiny, familiar to any student of myth, is that it is still a product of choice. You can lose it. It can be taken from you. Nothing had the right to take that from her. No one did. She ceased all communication with her mother.

✦

NOT THAT THIS WAS the first time they had stopped speaking. During her adolescence it was not uncommon for her to spend weeks at a stretch with her father and long-suffering stepmother after some eruption, and they'd had no contact for the entire semester following the George incident. But reconciliation always followed eventually, either through the intervention of a family member or the natural caving process. It stood to reason this process would repeat itself after the girl decided her mother had been punished long enough; Diane had made the mistake of instructing her too well in the embargoing of affection. Things were different this time, however. Her trips home had grown less frequent after graduation—because of

*work, the girl told herself, and not the feeling of foreboding in
her stomach the idea of returning inspired—so over the last few
years the decline in her mother's condition was conspicuous in
time-lapse. It didn't matter anymore how much of this was
psychosomatic: it was real enough Diane had put on two
stone at least, her complexion sallower with each visit, she
complained of the toll walking even short distances took on
her ankles. And the girl couldn't help but notice her mother
had stopped wearing short sleeve shirts, the wrinkled squares
of wax paper in the garbage can. She told herself her delay in
forgiving her mother was in proportion to the severity of the
offense, and not this feeling in her stomach she refused to call
disgust, that she was not the changeling of family mythology—
inhuman in her frigidity toward her mother's suffering.*

*The following fall the girl was in town staying with
her father for a wedding on his side of the family when a
horrific news story came out about a rape by the waterfront.
An unidentified woman had been held down and brutally
assaulted by multiple attackers. When this sort of story comes
out on a gloomy Pittsburgh November day it can only make
you question the point of anything at all. But in this instance
the case was cracked almost immediately. Apparently the
woman—whose identity was still withheld for her protection—
had fabricated the entire thing and performed the assault on*

herself with a glass Coke bottle. The girl and her father looked at each other wordlessly. It was impossible not to wonder.

Before she returned to New York they were called on by a woman who in this city would best have been described as "queer." She was in her fifties and morbidly overweight and very white, nearly albino, nearly translucent. She wore a shapeless dress that covered her up completely, but the girl imagined all the veins in her body were as visible as blue ink. Her manner was so timid that the girl imagined a harsh word from others would cause her to shatter; she reminded her of the ghosts in the Super Mario game that the girl would play with Mark in undergraduate, the big round ones who would sneak up on you but when you turned to them, face-to-face, would turn away with unbearable shyness. She said she was a friend of Diane's. Her father asked the woman what she wanted and she nearly flinched at the firmness in his voice. The girl felt bad for her but also good; there had been a limited number of times she'd ever seen her father protective of her. After all that time Diane had spent on the alliance between them, she was bringing the girl and John Kelly closer together. She would surely have been gratified by the echoes of Greek tragedy. The woman said that Diane didn't know she was here; that she would be upset if she knew. She would certainly enjoy pretending to be upset, *the girl did not interject. The woman continued that Diane had been having health problems—the girl and her father shared a look*—and had not been thinking straight because of the pain. *She had gotten herself into a sticky legal situation. The girl and her father looked at each other again.* He said he regretted to hear that, but neither of them were in a position to contribute financially. *The woman brushed right past this. Had she acted surprised or embarrassed by the reference to money the girl's suspicion of some sort of con would have been raised, but she was coming to believe she was simply a well-meaning kook Diane had gotten her hooks into. Another suspicion emerged that there may be more to this "friendship" and she realized she hoped this was true; it would be a relief to her omnipresent filial/Catholic/survivor's guilt to think her mother was not alone. The woman went on.* She knew that Diane had done much in the past that she was sorry for, and could not herself understand the reasons. You can go on Wikipedia and look up the term "malignant narcissist," *the girl did not interject.* "Until now," *said the woman portentously. The trouble Diane had gotten herself into had awakened something in her, something long forgotten, something that explained it all. Her voice had dropped to a hush. The girl steeled herself for disappointment: how disappointing it would be if, in the end, Diane became a Scientologist.* When Diane was a little girl, *explained the woman, her Sunday school teachers had actually been Satanists who committed abuses on her and forced her to commit ceremonies of an unspeakable nature and she had* buried all memory of it until this day. The woman looked at them wide-eyed at the scope of this revelation.

The girl and her father thanked her for this information. The girl told the woman she would pray for Diane.

✦

THE FOLLOWING MONTH THE girl was cutting through a park near her apartment when she was struck by the sight of a street lamp flickering to life and then extinguishing, like a glowworm in a jar. There is a porous border between sundown and the night, things slip through—it was her nature to know these things. This vision's meaning was as clear to her as if it was a message from the mysterious realm that had supposedly heralded her birth: someone close to her was going to die. The call from her father came the next day. Indeed, Diane had cleaned up her act, improving her diet and cutting junk cold turkey. But one side effect of quitting heroin is narcolepsy, and Diane had nodded off with a multivitamin in her mouth, which lodged in her throat, causing her to asphyxiate. Her mother was dead.

The girl received this news while she was in a taxi going down a narrow street. There was another taxi ahead of them, which stopped to discharge a passenger, and her driver honked *aggressively. This behavior had always struck the girl as odd—that no one was less generous to taxi drivers than other taxi drivers. She looked out the window where steam was issuing from a grate in a sidewalk, an effect that she liked; as alienating as the city could be, it created the impression it was a single breathing organism. On the other end of the line her father believed her lack of reaction was because of shock, and not the truth, that the girl had never been shocked less in her life.*

the click

EXACTLY ONE YEAR LATER I passed Jason in the lobby of the graduate library. He was leaving. We nodded curtly in passing.

I said, "Hey."

He stopped.

"I need you to be tall," I said.

He walked with me into the stacks to pick up a book I needed. It was on a high shelf and he reached for it and as he did his shirt rode up revealing the hem of his boxer briefs and the curve of his spine. He handed me the book and we looked at each other.

"Thanks," I said. There was a thin, hot film over my eyes.

"Are you okay?" he said.

"I'd be more okay with a drink," I said.

"Okay," he said.

In a few years, after neither of us live in Texas anymore, there will be a shooting on the same floor of the library. It will be of little consequence, as these things go. Some kid will shoot off a few rounds of an AK-47 in the stacks but won't hit anyone. His heart won't be in it. To be fair, I don't know where exactly it will happen, but when I hear about the shooting, I will decide it is on the same floor. When this story breaks I will be working for a Condé Nast ASPIRATIONAL LIFESTYLE MAGAZINE, profiling a San Francisco–based designer in a hotel bed with floor-to-ceiling windows over the bay and another irrelevant man on the other side of the bed because I will not be able to think of a lonelier situation than spending an expense account alone. I will read the story which will have been sent to me by a couple of former classmates and I will think of the hem of Jason's boxer shorts and the curve of his spine, and of Hogwarts, and the distinguished tradition of the mother institution of which Hogwarts is part of—sad young men announcing their grief with guns—and all the hurt in the world will seem mysteriously and incontrovertibly fucked, and I will close my laptop and look out the window and start to cry, wondering how many Condé Nast girls there are at that moment looking out the window of a hotel room and crying over a man she can never get back.

Jason and I went to a fratty sports bar just off campus that was close and cheap and sat in a corner booth with whiskeys and ice. I took a big swallow.

"There it is," I said.

"There what is," he said.

"The click in my head that makes everything feel more peaceful," I said.

We drank fast, saying little. I put my hand on the table. He put his hand on mine, once again running his finger on the indenture of my injured thumbnail.

"Let's go somewhere," I said.

"Where?" he said.

I didn't know. We had changed locations once already. But it felt like being on a bicycle, drunk, and the only imperative was to stay in motion.

We took a shuttle up to north campus, stopping at a 7-Eleven and got a very cheap wine with a screw-off lid, and from there he walked me to a fenced-in field with a few scattered dark oaks. He passed the bottle through the bars of the fence gave me a boost to climb over and then followed. He wanted me to notice his effortless physicality as guys do climbing fences, but I looked at the sky. Sunsets in Texas look like every kind of heartbreak you've ever had, one on top of the other. We walked to an oak on the outskirts of the field. I noticed rows of markers in the ground, only a handful and off-center, like an afterthought.

I said it looked like a cemetery.

"It is," said Jason. "It's where they bury the John Does from the mental hospital."

"How many nineteen-year-old communications majors have you finger-banged here?" I said.

"Shut up," he said.

Pleased, I unscrewed the cap from the bottle and took a drink.

"Tell me everything you like about me," I said.

"You have probably the prettiest eyes I've ever seen," he said.

I scoffed. "Everyone has pretty eyes."

"Is there a right thing for me to say?" he said.

"No."

He gestured for the wine and took a pull. "I think about you all the time. When people say your name it makes my stomach hurt. The other day I ran into Mark when I was getting lunch. We got a bagel together and had a completely harmless conversation. Every time I opened my mouth I just heard static. I can't even make myself jealous of him. All I felt was sorry."

"Why?" I said, irritated he wasn't jealous.

"Because he followed you down here and you don't love him anymore."

I got up.

"Where are you going?" he said.

I walked to the fence. He followed, repeating the question.

"I'm leaving," I said.

I looked at the fence and realized it was too tall for me to climb without his help.

"Help me up," I said.

"Tell me what I said."

"We're all at Hogwarts because we're insightful people," I said. "But you having insights into this that make it real, and you have no business making this real, you fucking idiot."

He was quiet. "What's Hogwarts?" he said.

"Help me over the fence," I said.

"No."

"If you don't I'll scream."

He stepped forward and reached past me with both arms and grabbed the bars of the fence, boxing me in.

"Scream," he said.

I wrapped my arms around his waist and lay my head against his chest. His heart was beating fast. He didn't know how fast my heart was beating, the advantage was mine. He stroked the top of my head. It was the first time I'd been touched like this by a body that wasn't Mark since

I was nineteen. I could smell his underarm mixed with his deodorant, the dank sweetness. I found his nipple with my lips and bit hard enough for him to gasp. He gripped me by both shoulders and said, "What is *wrong* with you?"

"I hate you," I said.

He looked at me, afraid, the way men do sometimes when they don't know if it's normal female stuff or if you're actually dangerously crazy. I have always enjoyed that look, probably the way boys do when they are holding guns. He lowered his face to mine. I turned my head and walked back to our tree and sat, picking up the wine. He sat next to me and we passed the bottle back and forth. He put his hand to the back of my neck and tried to kiss me again.

"Jason," I said, averting my face.

He pressed on. I put my hands to his face, pushing him off.

"Jason."

"You *bit* me," he said.

I laughed. Was that possibly true? We drank some more wine and he didn't make another move so I rubbed his thigh and left my hand there. He tried to kiss me again, and I resisted. I could feel him physically shuddering with frustration. It was very satisfying.

"Jason, *no.*"

He pulled back, breathing heavily through his nose.

"What?" I said.

"You said no," he said.

"I thought you were *fun*," I said. "I should have called Harry."

He put his hand on my face. It felt like sheet lightning spreading inside the skin of my cheek.

"Please come back," he said.

I pulled his arms around me and shook for a while, then it passed.

"My mother died a year ago today," I said.

He reached for the wine.

"When a thing like that happens, a thing like your mother dying, people expect you to feel shitty about it," I said. "This is the convention. And I do, I do feel pretty shitty about it. But I haven't told anyone the real reason why, not even Mark. At first I thought my reaction was numbness and that once I'd processed it, the things you're supposed to feel would kick in. Then some time passed and I realized that what I was numb to wasn't pain, it was relief. I didn't love her anymore. I hadn't loved her in years. My own mother. And her being gone felt like being set free, like some kind of permission for my life to really start. I haven't told anybody this so when they look at me they can see what they want. They have no idea what a monster I am on the inside."

His expression was blank, almost like he hadn't heard me. He drank again.

"I was being fancy earlier," he said. "I also like your ass."

I took him by the ears and pulled his face close to mine.

"I'm going to tell you something else, and it's very important, okay?" I said. "You have wings. You have a beautiful pair of wings; they are made of light. But they are broken. Your wings are broken. Do you understand what I'm saying?"

The sun was gone. The sky was all shocks of reds and pinks like we were inside of something alive.

"Okay," he said.

gardens

O N NEW YEAR'S EVE a group of us went to a party. Mark was my plus one. He had provided a notable lack of impediment between Jason and me so far, a result of his willful obtuseness to my emotional swings and having largely extricated himself from my new social life. A similar instinct, I suppose, as when an animal knows it's going to die. But he was bolstered by the results of a poker game before the party. This was an enthusiasm of his, the nocturnal hours he spent playing online while I was in the bedroom thinking of another man was probably the only comfort in his life. Poker night was naturally a

Harry initiative, so its purpose was of tense and unrelenting competition over camaraderie, thus an even sweeter victory to Mark when he took the pot. He crowed privately to me how he had "schooled those fools," a light in his eyes that had been no scarcity when we were a little younger. Like his ineffectuality in other masculine pursuits, gambling held no interest for Jason, and Mark was too happy to be curious how we had been occupying ourselves during his victory. And hopelessly oblivious to my own happiness that we were both beating Harry.

Earlier in December Harry had sat Jason down and told him quite earnestly that ambition, true ambition, consisted of terminal dissatisfaction. Contentedness is not the endgame of ambition, it is an affliction of *want*, to be found in perhaps one out of ten or twenty in a given population, and while it is possible for friendship to emerge between those similarly afflicted (but even this is thorny: see Hemingway's resentment of Fitzgerald or Franzen's of Wallace), a romantic relationship is impossible. Because an equal partnership is no more possible than between a garden and a gardener. Relationships don't exist between gardens.

"Wait, wait, wait," I interrupted the recounting of this conversation. "How much does he know?"

"He doesn't know anything."

"You *can't* be talking about this, do you understand?"

"Jesus Christ, of course I'm not talking about it. He just knew something was up between us and he was reading the tea leaves."

"Are you sure about that? Are you *sure* he was only reading tea leaves? Because you have a *very* big mouth and it would make me *very* unhappy if you were using it to turn this into a story."

"I'm not an idiot."

"Are you *sure* about that?"

"He doesn't know anything."

We were both lying. His was self-evident. He had the biggest mouth in the world and half the reason men have sex in the first place is for the story. Mine, characteristically, was much more subterranean and abstruse. As much as I was insisting on the motions of not getting caught, I still sat next to him at group outings and held his hand under the table. When he did not sit close enough to me I would engage him in petulant text exchanges—any observant person, of which Hogwarts almost entirely consisted, could detect the rhythm of the two of us picking up our phones. One great source of fun was to establish that an assignation's cue would be my departure from the group but then delay leaving until he was bursting with frustration, only to later chastise him for his obviousness. Being in love is the most charismatic hell. You watch every layer of sense and accountability fall away until you are reduced to a state of infantile helplessness, helpless to reason with your feelings, helpless to feel anything less than all of it. It's a gap in continuity, a wrecking digression: the self is a narrative, a certain number of events in sequence that being in love obliterates—this narrative imploding into a tormented present tense that you would choose to relive continually for the rest of your days if you could. And, without a doubt, I wanted Harry, my chief rival, to know about it, giving him taunting glances, mutually aware of my territorial victory, of how much he hated that there was nothing he could do about it.

"He cannot know a single thing; do you hear me?" I said.

Anyway, the party. Early on Jason began chatting with an Amazon girl who came to nearly his height in heels, with whom he made incremental progress over the night. I was beside myself. Literally, I was beside myself, that way your wrath actually becomes a separate and autonomous entity from yourself, then you become your wrath. He went to refill their red plastic party cups at a drinks station near a life-size statue of that Steve Buscemi–looking goblin thing from *Lord of the Rings* in a diaper and sash and holding a light-up party scepter. I made my way next to him and said, "She's not even that pretty. She's got a snaggletooth and she probably bought that dress at Target."

He didn't say anything.

"Like I even care," I said. "There's tons of cuter girls here, is all I'm saying. I don't care."

"It's good to know you're watching out for my interests," he said.

"You're only doing this to me because she's *tall*," I said.

He walked away. I followed. We had been together an hour ago, unknown to the others in our party. There is no greater bonding agent than conspiracy, which requires a more complicated but durable kind of honor. But now he was transparently curating his moment at the countdown with this Amazon whore.

He was CURATING in front of me.

"Are you punishing me?" I said.

"Are you leaving with me?" he said.

"I thought that maybe we were a little bit more *considerate* of each other than that."

"No, you thought you had two boyfriends for the price of one."

The conversation was dangerous. We were standing too close to each other and anyone could have recognized it as people who just fucked having a fight.

I felt a hand on my arm pulling me away. It was Harry. He asked what I was doing.

"I just think he can *do better*," I said. "What's wrong with a little *quality control* this day and age."

"It was a rhetorical question. Manage your shit."

"Does it bother you that I'm the one sucking his cock?" I said.

He looked at me.

"Did my dad teach you that look?" I said.

"Have pity on one of them," he said.

I remembered suddenly that Mark, abandoned to classmates across the room, still had eyes that worked regardless of how inconvenient it was for me. I had not really forgotten this, and I hated Harry perfectly for reminding me.

I returned to Mark and went through the motions of talking about the futility of resolutions and wasn't it crazy we were so close to the future in *Blade Runner* and so on. A playwright started talking about showing the novel he was working on to a contact at *The New Yorker*. Harry took some pleasure in explaining to him the unreality of this effort. This playwright had recently taken his first fiction class in which he demonstrated clear talent for the medium, and had been so inspired by the experience he'd written a full manuscript in several months. Equally vexing to Harry, this classmate was what was referred to as "Austin straight:" effete and sexually ambiguous but identifying as hetero, with a high degree of romantic success because he was as unthreatening as the scarves he wore in warm weather.

"That's cool, man, but *The New Yorker* won't really consider your shit unless it's submitted through an agent," said Harry. He had a spreadsheet of literary magazines and his own submission history on his computer, and currently led the fiction writers in publications, having placed stories in the *Paris Review* and *One Story*. "You wanna aim a little lower, and, honestly, it's a mistake to be showing these people unpolished work."

"Oh, he loved it," said the playwright. "He's showing an excerpt he thinks might work out to the fiction editor."

I enjoyed the look on Harry's face, but only fleetingly. Jason and the Amazon were sitting on a couch, and her knee was touching his like our knees had touched in the movies, and she was looking at him starry-eyed like he was telling her that the kind of life you live is the story you tell yourself, and all I could think about was the impending countdown, how at the end of it he would take her in his arms and kiss her, and how badly I wanted to throw my champagne in their faces when it happened. My hands were shaking at the thought of it.

"Look at him. I can't believe what an idiot he is. Someone should warn that girl she is dealing with a literal sociopath. Can you imagine what pretentious nonsense she's falling for?"

The look Mark and Harry gave me revealed I'd been speaking out loud.

"Someone really should warn her."

The playwright moved the conversation to the role of "the novel" in the future. He was enjoying a more attentive audience as a result of the potential imprimatur of *The New Yorker*.

"I mean, what place will it have for a generation raised on iPhones?" he said.

I angled away from Harry and said what an *interesting* question that was, touching his arm.

"It's done, you know?" he continued. "Kids today just aren't wired for it. But that's kind of exciting in its own way, you know? To be part of, like, a dying medium."

"You know what I think when people start talking about 'the novel'?" said Harry.

"What's that?"

Harry punched him in the mouth.

After Jason and I escorted Harry from the party and saw him off on his motorcycle, the two of us were left on the street.

"Should he be driving that thing?" I said, not hiding my scorn. I was being a drunk grotesque, so it was a pleasure to have someone who was more of a drunk grotesque to be better than.

"What if you stayed the fuck out of it? What would happen?" said Jason.

"Oh, don't worry, I don't have a single opinion. But I do have a question for you."

"Does the question involve staying out of it?"

"Do you know what happens when you love someone who hates himself? Do you know what happens when he turns on you, which he will, eventually?"

"Do you really have this much trouble with a simple request?"

"I'm just asking if you've thought about it."

"Is there some kind of mental block that makes you incapable of this one thing? Because who my friends are, or who I may or may not fuck later, or where she may or may not have bought her dress, are all equally none of your fucking business."

"FINE. I'm unbelievably fine with everything you're saying. I'm going inside."

I walked a few steps, but he didn't try to stop me so I turned back.

"Was it true you hadn't jerked off thinking about me?" he said.

I pretended not to know what he was talking about.

"When we were playing Truth. You said you hadn't masturbated thinking about me. Was it true?"

"What are you even talking about? It was a stupid game. This is the most retarded thing I've heard come out of your mouth, and that's saying *a lot*."

"Just answer the question."

"Yes, it was true."

"No, it fucking wasn't!"

"Simmer down."

"You can't play a game called Truth and then lie."

"I'm really glad this conversation isn't being recorded so you won't ever have to hear how retarded you sound right now."

"And you're lying now! I've still got your come on my dick and you can't admit this basic fact even now!"

"Simmer down."

"Tell me to simmer down again and see what happens."

"Big talker."

"Your boyfriend is watching us."

I turned to the house. Mark was standing in the glass to the side of the door, looking out with confusion. I could not believe he was still confused by anything in the universe. The look on his face made me understand how a person could take pleasure in kicking a dog.

"He's my *fiancé*."

I went inside, brushing past Mark and saying something about what idiots those guys were, I needed to make new friends.

I drank more champagne, and commiserated with the people encouraging the playwright that he should really think about pressing charges, and pretended not to be monitoring Jason and the Amazon, and visualizing her shocked sputtering whore face as my champagne hit it with the vividness of a movie you've seen a hundred times. As midnight approached we were all corralled out to the back deck where there were several old broken toilets; the house was situated over a ravine and there was to be a ceremonial clearing of the shit from the previous year. The owners of the house hoisted the first toilet onto the railing in preparation. The music playing was skipped to the intro of the Katy Perry song "Firework," timed so the chorus would kick in at midnight exactly. When the countdown started I shouted along with an ebullience to match everyone else's, or exceed it. I was reminded of a screenwriting term Jason used—"the ticking clock"—a climactic, tension-generating device often manifesting as the literal timer of some weapon of mass destruction that the hero must disable. *Five!... Four!... Three!...* I rooted for the hero's failure, more than ready for everything to be blown apart.

The toilet was flung into the ravine below, breaking apart on the rocks. Jason swept the Amazon into his arms. Mark reached to sweep me in his arms, but I pulled away. There was a frenzy of movement inside the house, then a thickly muscled dervish burst out on the deck. It was Harry. He had stripped down to his boxer briefs and was wearing the Baby New Year sash from the Steve Buscemi goblin. The scepter was in his hand, lights strobing, and his arms were pistoning and his hips gyrating to the music with abandon. His reappearance was met with peels of raucous and disbelieving laughter, even by those who had been advising legal recourse. There was the shattering sound of another toilet hitting the rocks. Harry's hands were now on his knees and he was grinding his rear into the crotch of the playwright, who gamely thrust in return, taking the wand and slapping it against Harry's haunch. It filled me with fury that somehow Harry's grotesquery was making him *more* popular. Jason stood with his arm around the Amazon, staring in great merriment at this display, her head bent into his chest, shoulders quaking. I had visualized at such length and intensity throwing my champagne in their faces, the undulating O shape of the whore's mouth as she searched for a reaction, that I barely noticed the distinction between the scene playing in my head and the reality as it came to pass.

✦

THREE DAYS LATER, MARK was on the road back to his parents' house in the Hudson Valley. There is not a word for the look in someone's eyes when you tell them you don't love them anymore. Jason was in a state. Mark had broken my phone in the aftermath of the party and by the time he left I was all used up. I was receiving several long emails of frantic eloquence from Jason a day; he did not know what was going on apart from a terse response from me not to come over and it was killing him, as it does when you are powerless to affect the outcome of a situation and can only assume it has gotten away from you. But his pain, so preventable by simple communication on my part that I would be on his doorstep soon enough (file under: be careful what you wish for), and Mark's pain, formerly so preventable by the smallest courage to tell him that following me across the country was such a bad idea that in the weeks before leaving New York I would wake up at night with my stomach in a knot, were both essential elements of the process that seemed reasonable to me: everybody had to hurt more than they needed to. Otherwise the process consisted of crying and binge-watching teenage TV melodramas on my laptop and pharmaceuticals that I was reminded to take again by the surprise of my teeth biting the quick of my fingernails.

A few days after Mark left I had a visitor. The thought it might be Jason angered me. I wanted nothing more than to

see him, but there was a process. Being angry at him was nice;
Galvan self-loathing is a magnet that will reverse polarity at
whim or convenience. But it was Harry.

"Well, isn't this some shit," he said.

"It is. It is most definitely some shit," I said.

He shook his head with a pleased grin. "Little shopper,"
he said.

"Was there something I can help you with?"

"Get out of your goddamn sweatpants. We're gonna
shoot some guns."

We went to an outdoor gun range east of the city where
the gas station had notepads for Bible study and bumper
stickers that said things like *Legalize Freedom*. At the range he
told me they still refused to allow Jews to become members,
then gave me a look that was either superiority that I fell
for it or that it shocked me, I couldn't tell which. After a
rudimentary lesson he held a dim view of my marksmanship.

"Your grouping pattern looks like it's been fucked by a
retarded child," he said. "Watch me. Your breath and your
shot are smooth and continuous. You've been to enough yoga
with your lesbo friends, the idea isn't foreign to you, shit just
blows up in the end."

He raised the gun and fired several rounds in a target
many yards further down from the one I had been shooting

at. Several shots went through the center mass of the black silhouette.

"In general it's preferred for targets to have more identifiable lifelike features, and to be moving rather than stationary," he said. "There is an instinctive human resistance to taking another life that could be the difference of having your face shot off in a combat situation if you haven't simulated it as closely as possible."

"You really, *really* would love a credible opportunity to shoot another human being," I said.

He fired several more shots into the target's head, and ululated in a Middle Eastern way. Then he reloaded the gun and gave it to me. I actually had been observing him and tried to emulate his calm concentration. I closed one eye.

"Keep both eyes open," he said.

"That doesn't feel right," I said.

"Well it is. You have to make your eyes sort of Chinese-y."

I squinted and my vision doubled, but I maintained focus on the front site between the doppelganger of my hands and inhaled slowly, and between the inhalation and exhalation pulled the trigger. I was still off by a mile, anticipating the noise of the recoil and jerking, but realized that the feeling of the gun in my hand as a loved and powerful part of myself and not an ugly man's toy was as good as I had felt lately.

"I'm having unbearable penis envy," I said, turning to Harry.

He cringed, taking my arms and steering them so the barrel pointed down range and not at his face.

"Finger off the trigger," he said. "Finger off the trigger."

Later, we took out our earplugs and collected the spent casings and dropped them in a plastic bucket.

"You're not the bad guy here," he said.

I looked at him, but he continued picking up casings.

"When my sadistic whore ex-wife completely emasculated me, she wanted nothing more than to have a baby," he said. "She didn't want her career to keep her from having a family and the agency was willing to let me go down to part time. But I was too selfish for that, and I knew it. What we do is the most selfish thing in the world. And I had years on my side, but she didn't, so she did what she had to. Could she have done it better? Yeah. So could I. So could everyone. People are a mess. People do shit to each other. Most of it is pretty understandable in their shoes and forgivable if it doesn't become a habit. So do me a favor and take it easy on the man cub. I have a lot of fondness for him, you know. But he is soft in a way that you and me aren't. It's not his worst quality."

I was surprised he was willing to admit the likeness between us. I didn't think he could say it about a woman.

His eyes lit then.

"Look at that," he said, and gestured down-range, but I couldn't see whatever I was meant to.

He walked onto the range a few yards out and pointed to a caterpillar in the grass, though it was unlike any caterpillar I had seen. It was green and totally smooth and very large like something out of the rainforest, at its plumpest nearly the circumference of my thumb. I would never have spotted it from the distance like he had, and realized that to do so required a degree of attunement to the natural world, which I secretly feared my lack of trivialized me as an artist.

His eyes lit again and he took a stick from the ground, which he used to pick up the caterpillar and run it to the dirt bank at the far end of the range, then jogged back, beckoning me.

"Oh, come on," I said.

But I followed and stuck my fingers in my ears as he sited carefully with a rifle and fired once. We walked again to the end of the range. What remained of the caterpillar was a spatter of incandescent green against the furrow of dirt like gemstones. I seized Harry's arm, unable to believe how pretty it was.

oh, the places you'll go

I N THE FALL OF the next year, his last at Hogwarts, Jason started working with a Hollywood manager. His script had placed decently in a screenwriting competition and this manager contacted him requesting a copy. Days later he called Jason in excitement, saying that the script had "X factor." Malloy was the manager's name; I don't recall his given name as Jason only ever referred to him as Malloy, or later "that Irish fuck." Malloy told him his script was "ninety percent there." Of course Jason and I were thrilled, as this could only mean he was going to be a millionaire next week. I came up with a logical argument to help Jason prepare for this windfall: it is said money does not buy happiness; thus, it can be assumed people are spending their money on things that don't make them happy; ergo, figure out the thing that makes you more happy than anything else and spend your money on that.

"I think that probably what makes me happier than anything else is…room service," I said.

"So really what we're doing is figuring out how to make *you* happy?" he said.

"Baby, let's be honest that your happiness pretty much depends on my happiness."

He didn't argue.

However, it soon became apparent that Malloy was not actually of woman born but had emerged from some dark, malign recess solely to be the bane of Jason's existence. Because their relationship existed exclusively by telephone, there were times I wondered if there was actually someone on the other end. In a place like Hogwarts where the apotheosis of success would have been to get a modest print run from Farrar, Straus and Giroux and appear on Terry Gross, Malloy was the archetype of profanity. Next week rolled into next month as "ninety percent there" became an endless series of notes and revisions. As an example, Malloy did not approve of abstractions, like when Jason explained a character's irrational bravado as stemming from a deep-seated fear of his own cowardice.

MALLOY: Slow down, college boy. Leo isn't afraid of being some kind of pussy. Leo eats pussies. What if…he tried to pull his wife out of a train wreck but the train exploded?

JASON: I'm not sure that's how steam engines work.

MALLOY: Then he could have a limp! No, a cripple is one step removed from being a pussy. He's addicted to painkillers!

JASON: Laudanum.

MALLOY: Huh?

JASON: If he was addicted to something it would probably be laudanum.

MALLOY (irritatedly indifferent): Details.

JASON: Details matter.

MALLOY (irritatedly indifferent): So he's addicted to *la de dah*. Then he's a cripple, but on the *inside*.

JASON: Doesn't that bring us back to the cowardice issue?

MALLOY: Yeah… (thinks) What if he had a kid who was there for the train wreck incident and went autistic?

JASON: I'm not sure that's how autism works.

MALLOY: But, I mean, *adoptably* autistic.

This process began the actual education, which Jason believed he'd been receiving in the academy, mainly in three lessons, hard earned. The first was the utter lack of irony with which the film industry regards itself; it is the perennial story that commerce feels zero onus to present itself as anything but self-parody to the artist. ("We have two modes, college boy: hustle and sleep. Are you sleeping right now?") The second was to fear more than anything the words "what if." That winter he spent hours and hours on phone conferences with Malloy, often sitting on the stairs outside my apartment, and I could tell when he heard those words because of the tremor that would run though his hunched shoulders like a beaten child. But this was where the rubber met the road. ("This is where the rubber meets the road," Malloy told Jason, as though sensing his verging tears of frustration.) It had always been Jason's ambition to be a Hollywood writer, but this was one thing relative to Hogwarts and another to Malloy; what Jason considered his own commercial instincts—honed as they were at the altar of Hitchcock and the Hollywood New Wave—were in fact too elitist and esoteric for twenty-first century Hollywood. When challenged by Malloy for a movie he had liked *recently* Jason named a French gangster movie;

nothing too pretentious, just a stylish little thriller that happened to be in the French language. Malloy scoffed. "I watch movies before I go to bed, I don't want to *read*." The disdain with which he stressed the last syllable contained the third lesson, and possibly the most important for Jason in the last of his Hogwarts days: success in Hollywood meant writing for an audience that *did not like to read.* Once this clicked, Jason had it: where Malloy was resisting him was when he was using his intellect as a crutch.

"That Irish fuck isn't wrong," he said. "Part of me is still trying to win a philosophical argument. Fuck philosophy, what am I, a playwright? It's my job to find the good version of what he wants the moronic version of."

Thus the third rail was found between Jason's problematic literacy and Malloy's philistinism. If an element wasn't landing it was because Jason hadn't worked hard enough to find the solution his taste could countenance that still succeeded on the level of id. In the next draft Jason took all his pet philosophical ideas and refracted them into a more primal lexicon of *kiss kiss bang bang*, culminating in a third act consisting of an extended white-knuckle chase sequence that exhausted his thesaurus of synonyms for the word "run" (*barrel, bolt, bound, careen, carom, charge, dart, dash, etc.*)—which was by a mile the most impressive technical achievement he had produced yet, and, in a medium defined by kinesis, objectively improved the script.

"I will cut off my fingers before I ever write another character pondering his existential situation," said Jason.

"I think we have something really special on our hands," said Malloy.

By now it was April, and though the path here had been frustrating, as long as he became a millionaire before graduating he would be happy. Malloy told him he had an agent in mind who would be a good fit and indeed had given it "a rave," but it was nearly a month before Jason could get on the phone with her. This did a number on him. He tried to find meaning in why she kept rescheduling, but could accept none except the fraudulence of her interest, and fuel for his growing fear of having worked for six months with a man he had never met. I told him that based on my magazine experience sometimes months would go by before editors responded to a story that had been filed and he should try not to read into it. He didn't listen to me. He was incapable of listening to me, he was incapable of letting me help. It was no more in his power to climb out of Fort Jason than it was in mine to climb in. It did not improve things that Harry could.

"He says none of this is aboveboard," said Jason. "It's weird that I've been doing all this free work for this guy with no contract or transparency."

I now knew there was nothing I could do to alleviate Jason's paranoia. He had no personal experience of the business world so all Harry had to do was use grown-up words like TRANSPARENCY to exert ultimate authority over him. This precipitated a fight between us because this was all the confirmation I needed of the subtle and insidious chess game Harry was playing against me.

This pertained to another development that year, which was that the university had instituted a new student literary prize, which, in inimitable Texas fashion, was for nearly $100,000. The impact on Hogwarts was seismic, the knee-jerk reaction being snobbish disdain—what a gauche spectacle, a literary minstrel show—but this masked a grimmer truth. Because while the university had over fifty thousand students, it was obvious that this was a de facto Hogwarts competition, giving lie to the program's democratic auspices. The fact was, we were in a position of staggeringly undemocratic prestige relative to the mother institution, and in this womb we had become sharks. (Sharks are intra-uterine cannibals.) Nature is not a democracy. When this prize was announced I doubt Harry's erection went down for a week. His cult of social Darwinism had established a temple, finally there was something quantifiable to *win*.

Amplifying the offensiveness of this prize was its single mandate, to reward the work that best encapsulated

AMERICA IN MICROCOSM. *Sturm und Drang.* Could there have been a clearer message to emulate the Dead White Males whose palate-friendly dominion was so antithetical to why many of us were here in the first place? Could our ineffectual protests have hidden less how much all of us wanted that goddamn prize?

"That neck-less piece of shit is trying to get into my head," I said. "I mean, 'neck-less' as a physical attribute, not like jewelry."

"I'm following," said Jason. "But the math here is giving me trouble."

"He's trying to wind you up because he knows it will psych me out."

"Okay. I guess I don't see him as trying to wind me up, he's just trying to give me data points."

"Did you know that I hate that word? *Data points.* Because I really do. It's not that I hate it like *intrinsically*, like, *ontologically* it is fine, if a little crass. But I hate that word the way the two of you use it in your he-man woman-haters club sort of way."

"It's actually two words," said Jason.

"That happens in close romantic relationships, you know. Vocal mimicry. If an impartial third party were to hear recordings of the three of us talking, I wonder which two they would conclude were fucking."

"Are we honestly having a vocabulary fight?"

"This isn't a fight! Who said this was a fight! I'm just saying it would be an *interesting* experiment."

"Okay. I guess I don't see the sinister master plan in my friend giving me an unbiased *perspective* on a professional question."

"*Unbiased,*" I said with a laugh that I did not want to believe was a sound coming out of me.

"He just wants to help me. In the same way that, if the roles were reversed, I'd want to help him. It's a pretty astoundingly uncomplicated human impulse."

"If you ever helped Harry he would bite your hand off."

"Supposing the utter redundancy at this point of trying to poison that well, can we explore the radical paranoia of believing he's only doing it to get to you?"

"Exactly!" I punched him in the arm for strengthening my case. "That is exactly what his plan would be, because then if I call him out on it you just call me a crazy bitch and it's still a success."

"Jesus Christ, no one called you a crazy bitch. You called yourself that."

"You did. You called me a crazy bitch! But it's fine. It's fine, it's fine, it's fine. I know you've got a lot on your mind right now, so I wouldn't want my writing to be an inconvenience."

This was stooping. When I review the transcripts of some of the things I said to manipulate the given argument in my favor, there is plenty I'm not proud of; however, accusing him of wanting to fuck other girls or loving me less than the guy I left him for or loving his misogynistic neck-less piece of shit best friend more than me all fell into the category of fair play, by Galvan rules. But some things are sacred, and whatever we did to each other as a boy and a girl was separate from the simple goodness we did for each other as artists. We supported each other with a religious lack of question or condition. Even the oblique incrimination that he was treating me like a GARDENER went to the quick, and, seeing that woundedness in his eyes from this low tactic, I wanted nothing more than to hold and comfort this sweet boy who after all this time still did not understand why I would hurt him like that, as I looked at him with the savage smugness of a Galvan holding the whip.

"Can you please explain to me what the point of psyching you out would be when the stories are already in the process of being judged?" said Jason.

"Irrelevant. You know how competitive he is. You know that *Art of War* shit he's into. He's so afraid of losing to me that he would try to get into my head just so that's what I was *putting into the universe.*"

Jason considered this. "You are being a crazy bitch," he said.

"You'll see. When you learn what a mistake it was to be loyal to him over me I want you to remember something. I forgive you. Okay? Remember that I forgive you for what you're bringing on yourself."

"I guess I'm done with this conversation," said Jason, deflated in a way that meant I wasn't even going to get mean sex out of this.

"I forgive you, baby," I said.

Of course he was also getting the same from the other side.

"She's undermining you," Harry told him (in my mind—though I was hardly imagining things). "You think she wants you to be successful, but that's the last thing she wants. And if she thinks there is the danger of you becoming the player that we all know you're meant to become, she is going to drop a nuclear warhead on it. Because rich, young Hollywood ballers don't marry their alcoholic train wreck grad school girlfriend."

But tensions diffused when Jason finally got this agent on the phone. It was a ruby slippers moment: the entire point of the call was to determine whether or not Jason was interested in working with *her*. She and Malloy agreed that the ideal strategy would be to take the script out the first week of May.

"Apparently, it's when the studios are just starting to get their beaks wet with summer money. They're primed," said Jason at a celebration group outing that night. The pleasure he took in speaking knowledgeably about industry workings was like a child in his father's lap pretending to drive the car.

I was surprised by how happy I was. Of course I knew I would be happy for him, Harry was offensively wrong on that score, but the pride I felt for him was alarming, narcotic, possessive, queasy; he was lucent, a comet in reverse—no wake, but trajectory searing. He had a destiny. There is no feeling to match the ferocious pride you feel for someone whose genitals have been in your mouth.

"I guess all the rescheduling was just because she was busy," said Harry. "In the future we should remember that the stakes for us are completely different than the stakes for them, and it's impossible to read into anything."

"Hindsight is twenty-twenty," I said, not observing that this was the exact point I had been making when Harry had been driving Jason out onto the ledge. Though I was over the idea that doing so was part of Harry's strategic campaign against me—if I had even believed this accusation myself as much as needed Jason's concession he was *capable* of it.

It is winter. I go to bed with running clothes on so when I wake up I can be moving instantly, propelled outside, teeth hurting in the cold, face florid red, the only color in the landscape. I do this as an insurance policy that I will get out of bed. It should be tranquil, the streetlamps go out and the violet of dawn becomes the blue of day, black snarl-tooth pilings emerging from the water, the only souls out this hour the gainfully employed and the elderly, evidence that civilization is on the rails. But for it to be tranquil would require it to be quiet, and that would require a different person's brain, one that didn't have the thoughts that are in mine, ninety-nine out of a hundred being resentments or regrets, flipping over each other like fish for crumbs. I try to focus on the one that is not pitying or destructive, the one that is curious without judgment about the variables that led to my present circumstances, that all the same would prefer not to repeat them, not to go through life as Diane II, martyr after all to her inability to identify how responsible she is for feeling how she feels. When these thoughts turn, as they often do, to Texas the most overridingly reasonable of them is bafflement over the things Jason and I fought over.

Imagine two stones dropped into a pond close together. When the resultant waves superimpose this is called an interference pattern. If the crest of one wave meets the trough of the other it flattens both, but if the reverse happens—peak-to-peak, valley-to-valley—the magnitude of displacement is equal to the sum of both magnitudes. We doubled each other, our best and memorable worst. She the manipulator addict by-product of a manipulator addict, he the autistically stubborn Texan whose gift for admitting he was wrong—or recognizing the moments when for the sake of all involved he should do so even if he didn't mean it—rivaled a penguin's for flight. So there was always something to torture him over, and, unlike Mark, he was incapable of getting me to stop by submitting until I felt sorry for him. As far as I was concerned his eye was always roving to some slut or whore in our social circle, the given object generally inspired less by plausibility or Jason's actual tastes, and more to proximity and whether she was skinnier than me. (Him: "You know that only crazy women call each other sluts and whores?" Her: "It's fine! If you want to fuck her, IT'S TOTALLY FINE.") I know now in a way it was impossible for me to know then how much it hurt him when I went so low as to give voice to my own darkest thoughts, using the worst word against myself. Him: "Ugly is an ugly word"—as if to a child, and I would scoff like a child, as if he wasn't right. I had a Charles Gilbert picture taped to the corner of my bathroom mirror, the image of a Victorian-era woman sitting in front of her own mirror creating the optical illusion of a grim skull with the caption: *All is vanity.* Him: "Do you honestly have no idea how awful that picture is?"

Not that he was blameless. His preferred method for dealing with vulnerability was avoidance, his biggest allergy was to compromise, and while he came to be even more aware of my triggers than I was, he would continually set them off out of what had to be masochistic boredom. He especially enjoyed telling stories about ex-girlfriends or sexual conquests, and when we were first together he had a pair of panties hanging from the rearview mirror of his truck. A PAIR OF PANTIES. He maintained that this was a design element independent of the panties' provenance, and that it wasn't a respect issue toward me one way or the other. A PAIR OF PANTIES. You idiot. Even he was smart enough to lose this one, eventually, after much blood loss.

The time smoking coolly in bed I pick a fight that makes him put his fist through my wall, not an inch from the crossbeam. I tell him to be careful, he writes with that hand.

The time driving down I-35 he loses himself in his favorite kind of anecdote—the triumphant adolescent sexual exploit kind—and I take his wrist and bite the fleshy part of his palm very hard. He shoves me, eyes wide with the desire to retaliate more, and points out we're going eighty miles an hour, as if it's relevant.

The time driving to his mother's house for dinner that I refuse to let up on whatever the day's offense is—my recollection doesn't extend to what it was, or whether it was real or imagined—and he feels so impotent to put on a nothing's-wrong face for his mother at the same time as fixing whatever impossible thing I need to be fixed that he pulls to the side of the road and screams at me till his voice cracks. That does fix things for me, a little.

The time he gets tired of a fight before I do and leaves in the middle of it to get drunk with Harry and I leave him eleven voicemails calling him a faggot.

Of course, roughly half our fights were about Harry, subtextually. No matter who I was accusing him of wanting to sleep with in a given moment there was no question who my actual enemy was. This went both ways. Harry hated that there was a part of Jason that would only belong to me and not him, just as much as I hated the opposite, and we made him suffer for it like a child of divorce who could not comprehend why he should be punished for loving who he loved.

Of course, roughly all our fights were about his plan to leave for Los Angeles when he graduated and became famous, as even his detractors knew was somewhat inevitable—or the only possible way for a Galvan to see it: his plan to leave me.

✦

THE SCRIPT WENT OUT on a Wednesday. This was a complicated process that Jason attempted to explain to me, and mostly consisted of feigning a blasé posture and qualifying things that should have been insanely exciting.

JASON: Leo's company loves it.

LEDA: Leonardo DiCaprio? That's amazing.

JASON: Not him, per se. His…people, I guess is the terminology.

LEDA: Are they going to buy it?

JASON: They're going out with it.

LEDA: I thought it went out already.

JASON: It did. To production companies. Now it's going out to territories.

LEDA: What's a territory?

JASON: A movie studio.

LEDA: What's the difference between a movie studio and a production company?

JASON: The studio is the bank. The producer's first job is to get a bank.

LEDA: Why do they say "territory" instead of just studio? It's actually more syllables.

JASON: To be less comprehensible, I guess.

LEDA: Well you have to be in good shape with LD producing your movie. I've decided to call him LD in social situations. I hope it doesn't compromise your professional relationship when he falls hopelessly in love with me.

JASON: They're not actually attached; they're just getting a territory. I think their deal is with Warners.

LEDA: Who's getting other territories?

JASON: I didn't know all of them. Bruckheimer has Disney. Rudin has Sony.

LEDA: Baby, this is unbelievably good news.

JASON: ...Potentially.

LEDA: What's not good about this?

JASON: It's not real yet.

LEDA: When is it real?

JASON: When there's money.

But as much as Jason tried to hide behind the newly acquired front of insider cool, he could not extinguish his excitement. Rudin, Bruckheimer—presumably there were irrelevantly mortal men somewhere attached to these names, but this was beside the point; his life had reached the threshold of the mythic dimension he believed he had been intended for. He was knocking at the door. The timing raised another possibility: if Jason sold this script he didn't have to move to Los Angeles.

This led to a very long weekend. *We live or die by Monday*, Malloy told Jason. But on Monday he did not, as he expected, wake up to news on *Deadline Hollywood* that his script was in the middle of a bidding war. He waited all day for his phone to ring, speculating uselessly on why it wasn't. The two-hour time difference, whether an offer would come in before or after lunch, whether they would call him until they heard from all parties, etc. He drove around fretfully listening to music at full volume. He went to the local independent video store and browsed every title, the ritualistic way he had to before making a selection. He rented nothing. His mind would not still. The entire time he wanted to call Malloy but restrained himself out of the same superstitious (and correct) instinct that calling someone you like first will make them stop liking you. But, as is always the case, Jason caved in the end, and called just before the end of business day, Pacific time.

MALLOY: What's up?

JASON: …Are we alive or dead?

MALLOY (a pause, chewing)

JASON (a pause, having an embolism)

MALLOY: Sorry, I'm eating. (swallowing sound) No one has passed.

JASON What does that mean?

MALLOY: It means no one has passed. They're getting their heads around it.

JASON: Getting their heads around what? It's a binary. What's so complicated about yes or no?

MALLOY (a pause, chewing): We live or die by tomorrow.

But this was not the case. Nor was it the day after, or the day after that. A pass or two came in, but for the most part the situation remained unchanged: multiple territories were interested, but none would make a move.

"It's a Mexican stand-off," Malloy told Jason. "Everyone's waiting for someone else to pull the trigger."

"But...if everyone really likes it, why won't anyone make a play for himself?" said Jason.

"They just need someone else to do it first to know how much they like it. Keep the faith, these knuckleheads will never let a spec with this much action on it pass them by. I guarantee we'll have a definitive answer by weekend."

But the waiting was taking its toll on Fort Jason; the walls were beginning to crack. He was tense and dislocated in conversation, and whenever his phone rang a jolt would run through him and his face would go from not wanting to be excited to annoyed with his own disappointment in less than a second. Eventually, he said he'd had enough and started to keep his phone on silent, which he stated was for his own sanity but I knew it was really for mine and he was checking it every time my back was turned. I was grateful for the consideration.

One night at dinner we ran into an old screenwriting professor of Jason's from undergraduate, the one who had sponsored his Hogwarts application. Jason gave him a rundown of the situation, hoping to get some perspective.

"You know," said the man, "this isn't going to be your last professional opportunity."

We sat down and Jason said, "That smug prick."

His tone was so bitter I could have been talking to my father.

"He wrote on *Law and Order* when the first Bush was in office and now he wants me to fail so it validates his own failure. Harry is right. They're all fucking vultures who feed on failure."

"Who is 'they'?" I said.

"Fuck him," said Jason.

"I was standing right there. I didn't see what you're seeing. Jason, you're twenty-three years old. I think he was just trying to say this isn't the end of the world."

"Are you really saying that? Are you *really* trying to say to me this *isn't* the end of the world?"

Though he was not raising his voice, it was still upsetting to see him this unhinged. But I tried not to let it get to me. So often it was me going off and Jason reigning me in that I told myself it was now his turn. I would take care of him like he took care of me.

"Baby, I know this is really hard on you, but what you're doing is called ruminating, okay? It's the way cows digest, it just keeps passing from stomach to stomach and it's not getting you anywhere, it's just turning more and more into shit. You need to stop thinking about it, okay? I know that's so much easier to say than to do, but you have to try really hard to think about other things."

"I agree with you. That would certainly be the enlightened approach to this. But there is a complication, which is that when I'm successful at silencing my brain and not *ruminating* on this topic, a sound fills the silence. It is like I'm alone in a vast cave with the deafening sound of *chewing* echoing in my ears."

"You tell me what there is for me to do to help you."

He was quiet.

"I think the thing only you can do is…let this happen and still be here when it's over."

I took his hand and kissed it.

✦

No answer came the next day. It never did. Another week passed and it sunk in that nothing was going to happen. Everyone had waited on everyone else until they forgot what it was they were waiting on.

"Goddamn spec market," said Malloy, finally throwing in the towel. "This was the nineties you would have had a seven-figure sale and an overall deal."

"That is good information," said Jason. "Thank you."

"Would it make you feel better if I told you you are going to be a fucking star?"

"…Somewhat."

"Then get your ass out here so I can make you a fucking star."

✦

Jason's class graduated, but his eyes were on the horizon. He lined up a subletter for his apartment in Austin and was hitting up Craigslist to get a sense of the LA market. This was daunting. He had saved up enough to live half a year by Austin standards but saw that this wouldn't go nearly as far in Los Angeles.

And, inevitably, Harry won the prize. I knew it was coming. The night before it was announced I had dreamed of receiving a phone call from the prize committee, but upon answering a vomitous torrent of black bile issued from the phone. I sent him a congratulations text the next day just before receiving the actual news. Though he was conserving money for the move, Jason presented him with an expensive bottle of Scotch at the celebratory drinks. Harry was sitting at the end of the table wearing a plastic tiara. Jason stood behind him with his hands on his trapezii, kneading.

"I didn't know it was possible to be this happy for someone and this furious," said Jason.

"Bottle it," said Harry. "No plan B. I lived my plan B for ten years and turning my back on it was only possible by having every vestige of my manhood served to me on a plate. Now is the time. You have nothing to lose."

But Jason didn't need the encouragement. Though this process had been painful, it was the waiting far more than the outcome. The defeat only primed him for the fight. It was a turn-on. It is a highly satisfying feeling to see your man is up to the task. This was the first major test of Jason's idea of who he was and what he was capable of, and his recovery time from heartbreaking disappointment to packing his suitcase was nearly instantaneous. I was even prouder of him in defeat than I had ever been of his terrific promise, this preview of the man he was becoming.

So this is how I showed him.

✦

ONE EVENING IN MID-MAY, Jason came by to discuss arrangements. At the time I was dog-sitting for a friend. Though growing up my home situation was never stable enough to own a pet, historically the animal kingdom has been overly attached to me. Stray cats come to me in the streets eager to rub deposits of musk, and my presence has been known to cause great consternation in the primate house of the Pittsburgh Zoo. It is my theory that this is how the concept of the witch's "familiar" came to pass: some of us are simply selling what they're buying. Zion, a large malamute, was no exception to this trend. There was none of the separation anxiety typical of dogs removed from their home and master; he could hardly have been happier in my care. Except when Jason was around. It was funny: under other circumstances the dog liked Jason well enough, but as soon as he started staying with me, Jason's presence in the apartment would make Zion surly and possessive—barking and growling aggressively at his arrival and sulking once chastised, keeping me between him and Jason while giving furtive resentful looks. "Mad-dogging me, fuckin' dog is mad-dogging me," Jason would insist. I would pretend it was all in his head, preventing myself from smiling. And the ruckus the brute made when these visits took a turn for the carnal! He would howl such a storm when Jason touched me we would have to lock him up in the bathroom to prevent him from damaging any furniture, and the dire yelping and scratching that would follow made concentrating on the act itself nearly impossible. At one point Jason became so frustrated he stopped mid-coitus and stormed to the bathroom, throwing open the door with the intention of staring the dog into submission: a hierarchy had to be established. But before Jason had the opportunity to assert his dominance the dog shot past him with unexpectedly feline cunning, seized my panties from the floor, and settled into the corner with a defiant grip on his prize.

"Nice. Very nice. We're definitely sending a consistent message here," said Jason.

But how could I stop laughing? What more buoying feeling is there than when there is not enough of you to go around?

This was the situation when Jason and I were walking the dog and solidifying our agenda for the drive as dusk settled this May evening, the prettiness of it auguring that same shipwreck feeling I'd felt back when we were in the lunatics' cemetery, the beauty possessing a flair for the apocalyptic. The plan was for me to drive out with him and then fly from Los Angeles. It was a straight shot from the 10 but we were going to allow ourselves a few extra days to make things more interesting.

"I've never seen the Grand Canyon," he said. "I mean, F for originality, but what are you gonna do—it's the fuckin' Grand Canyon. And Susan and Jeff are in Santa Fe. She's teaching at that hippie school where all they do is read good books instead of learn. Was also thinking in California we could go check out the Winchester House. Do you know that one? It's this mansion that's like a crazy labyrinth with no building plan, no windows, and stairways to nowhere. The story is the widow of the Winchester fortune was convinced that the family was cursed by the ghosts of everyone who had been killed by a Winchester rifle, and required the house to be perpetually under construction."

I nodded vaguely at whatever he was saying, distracted by the swishing of Zion's bushy tail, reminding me of a feather duster. It was a monologue in my direction, not a conversation; it passed through my ears like the cries of the grackles. This trip was nothing more than a metaphor for the world of possibility lying ahead of him.

"Are you okay?" he said.

"Sorry, baby," I said. "I'm good. That all sounds really good. I can't wait."

He smiled. The smile of a boy with feet itching to take him on the adventures waiting for him. If I'd proposed we throw bags in his car and leave in that moment he would have been thrilled.

He went on with ideas for the road trip.

The dog stopped and crouched. I looked off. My sense of shame was so profound it even extended to feeling discomfort on behalf of animals. I had come from squalor and refused to allow it to reclaim me. I caught my own reflection in the window of a parked car. She was recrimination incarnate. *Is that what you think?* her eyes said. I put on my sunglasses and pulled a ziplock bag over my hand. In my distraction it occurred to me something was different. Jason wasn't talking anymore. I looked at him and saw that he was in a condition I had literally never seen him in before. He was speechless. I smiled the way we do at things that are new and fearful.

He did not smile back. His features were ossifying in that familiar way.

"What is that?" he said, from somewhere inside Fort Jason.

I followed his pointed finger to the sidewalk. It is tempting in scenes like this to anthropomorphize the reactions of animals, but it is an even more obtuse exercise than attempting to understand each other, if that's even possible. The dog was as indifferent to us as it was to the human inheritance of shame, much less the pale, vermicular, indigestible passenger in its stool, an abhorrently ribald pig in a blanket.

The dog turd contained a used condom. One which hadn't been used by Jason.

✦

BY THE TIME WE reached the apartment the barometric pressure had dropped and the pink clouds had black wisps like cotton candy that had been held to a flame. As the saying goes: if you don't like the weather in Texas, wait five minutes. I poured each of us a whisky. He took it without saying anything.

"I want you to promise me something," I said. "Promise me that no matter what happens from now on you'll never let anyone make you smaller than you are."

I held my glass out to toast. He didn't meet it.

"Now your life starts," I said.

I moved my glass to meet his in a clink but he pulled it away, downed it in one swallow, and placed the glass on the counter with a sharp *clack*. Not anger, some form of punctuation.

"It was a nice idea," I said. "We were a nice idea, and it would be nice to pretend that there are not certain realities, but there are."

"Can you define 'certain realities'?"

"Do I really have to? How many autopsies have we had while we were still alive?"

We were both quiet.

"When I think of the places you'll go I get this crushing feeling like there's a thousand pounds on my chest," I said. "But I've gone as far as I'm going with you."

Zion was lying on the floor with passive anxiety over the turning weather. Jason sat on the couch and ran his hands up and down the fur of the dog's chest with quiet focus. I was aware that the absence of emotion on his face was a quirk of his brain and not an earnest attempt to spite me, that rather than evading this conflict he simply wanted one moment of shared mammalian warmth before whatever was going to follow, but as though on a television game show buying spree at this point my vengeance was pulling items from the shelf with abandon. I had never felt a closer bond with Diane: the annihilation of all sensible reasoning in submission to this cleansing wave of shadow.

"Tell me why," he said.

He did not know how unready he was for what he was saying, and I found his ignorance tiresome.

"Baby, read between the fucking lines."

"What lines? Can we establish a personal first and talk about what we're actually talking about?"

There was a raucous noise outside and something out the window caught my eye, two massive black wheels in the sky, one on top of the other, and parallel to the ground, turning in opposite directions. It was grackles flocking in discrete gyres.

Yes. I was ready to establish this personal first.

His hands went still in the dog's fur like he was pressing them into his star on Hollywood Boulevard. In the cacophony of the grackles Jason did not fully process my answer. Nor did he days later on the 10 driving alone and stopping only for rest station naps under the desert sky's overturned black colander, or when he reached the ocean and stood with pant cuffs rolled up and waves lapping his bare feet, or a long time after that. Not that all the signs hadn't been in front of

him. Every time. Every time Harry put me down in public
led to this. Every time he made me feel small. Every time
the voice inside my head that believed I wasn't talented
enough, or smart enough, or pretty enough, spoke to me in
Harry's voice. Every time Jason failed to make me feel loved
enough. Every time he succeeded. Every time he told me not
to call myself ugly. Every time he believed in himself, and
made me believe in him, shining too brightly, like someone
who would never need me, like someone who would leave
me. Harry had said at the gun range that we were alike in
ways that Jason was not like us. Mainly, we knew that this
was a world where the people who love you the most can do
this to you. The heart's inconstancy, its plasticity, above all
its capacity for treason to itself. That day the previous year
driving back from the range I curled up in the passenger side
and the top of my head touched Harry's leg and if he had
touched me back then I can't say how history would have
gone. He was tattooed and heavily muscled and smelled rank
and dangerous and knew how to fix things and kill things
and I had already protested far too much. But he didn't, then.
He waited. He was a satellite male always around to tell me
I wasn't good enough, until he was on the way up and Jason
was already out the door. I think in Harry's imagination he
was doing Jason a favor, setting his world on fire, giving him
nothing to come back to. It had happened several days ago.

I told Harry I needed him to look at a leaking faucet that obviously Jason would be useless for, and while I'm not sure either of us exactly planned it, it felt like if I'd passed my hand over my head I could have felt the strings. Squalor reclaimed its own. Perhaps it should be noted that Harry requested that nothing be said until after Jason's departure, that there was no point in shoving the knife in beforehand. But saying this was only words: he knew who was wielding the knife.

It would be a long time before Jason understood what a mistake he'd made trusting short people.

The object of this exercise is honesty. This was never my strong suit. And I don't know if I can ever send this to you, baby, because I'm still so mad at you.

Jason looked at me for a long time, those great black wheels turning in an ominous and inscrutable mechanism in the sky behind him; his eyes had already begun the search that was to define the next chapter of his life, the search to understand how he *possibly* hadn't seen this coming. I shrugged with polite helplessness and attempted to keep the giddiness from my voice. The process was simple. Everyone had to hurt more than they needed to.

"I'm not in love with you anymore," I said.

funny you should ask that, Terry

FUNNY YOU SHOULD ASK that, Terry. Three weeks. Harry and I lasted three weeks. His parting words to me were: "And that's my limit for being criticized by a woman." I didn't see him after that. He went to New York to meet an interested agent and wound up getting an apartment with his prize money. Not long after that there was a bidding war for his book, which he sold for an amount of money we will not discuss, as to this day the specific figure has the power to induce hives. He bought a house in the Adirondacks to kill beautiful things and tell himself stories around the campfire of his own greatness.

After he left, I walked to the lunatics' cemetery to have a cry. There was a strange hissing sound in the grass and I looked down and saw a tiny creature, a mammal of some kind no bigger than a mouse. I couldn't tell you what it was, really; it looked like the magical friend in a fantasy novel. If I'd taken another step I would have squashed it flat, but there it stayed, raising up on its hind legs and bristling and baring its teeth, hissing at me. I suppose I must have been approaching its burrow or whatever, but it gave no quarter! I crouched down and now this Lilliputian warrior was spitting mad, hopping and spreading its paws. I was so infatuated I forgot my heartbreak for a moment—my first instinct was to clutch Jason and show him. But Jason was gone forever. That was the first moment the reality of what I had done really caught up with me. I sat back on the ground, all the air left my body. I had lost the right to share the smallest wonders.

A vole, maybe? I don't know.

I finished my last years in Texas in a state of near neutrality to what my future held except the time and location of my first drink. The immolation of the body a consecration, every hangover a benediction. Or whatever crap writers use to turn cowardice into valor. I didn't actually write a word I wasn't repelled by. For every action there is a reaction, and it stood to reason I had been a party to destruction and thus had lost the gift of creation. But this was not the case. The news came to me that Jason had sold a movie pitch, and my imagination was never more fertile than it was conjuring scenarios for the glamorous new life he had left me for. (In these scenarios there was no ambiguity that HE had left ME.) Sometimes I would see a couple in public, the man resting his hand on the back of the woman's neck in a gesture I have always found so brutally tender it makes my heart fall into my stomach, or find myself running a finger along my own scarred thumbnail the way Jason used to, or some other small provocation I would use to listlessly sleep my way through a ring of some of his other friends who had stuck around. It was both over- and under-kill. Diane Galvan's daughter, the prophecy fulfilled, had been left behind.

At least Austin was a good city for that; a high degree of intelligence and planlessness were virtually prerequisites for residence. Musicians referred to it as "the Velvet Coffin"— you can live such a comfortable life there you will never be compelled to leave to start your real one. I got a job with an organic cleaning service—well, yes, that is another word for it: an eco-friendly maid. Terry, if you gave me a rag and some white vinegar you would not recognize this studio afterward! I didn't mind it. I'd spent so much of the previous years with status-obsessed males that I saw honor in servitude. Cleaning someone else's house is one of the great anonymous acts of love. Our customers were mainly in west Austin, all the tech industry nouveau riche. The things that people who can afford organic maids buy! Lawn gnomes in ten-gallon hats around koi ponds made of plastic rocks, all-white shag carpeting, chandeliers in the bedroom. But this was where the universe had directed my anonymous acts of love and it was not my place to question it. Freedom is the enemy of happiness.

In one of these houses there was a kid home from college: a skinny, entitled, resentful child passing through life with a perpetual sneer. He was always around when I was working and would make an exaggerated display of annoyance at my presence while managing to place himself directly in my path as much as he could: wanting to watch the particular television in the room I was cleaning or waiting until I was in the kitchen to become imperatively hungry. His eyes were small and he was acne-prone, yet the majority of available wall space was devoted to photos of him throughout his undistinguished academic and athletic career. Some empathy was required for an unphotogenic credit to no one entombed by the brittle fantasy of his mother. One day I was cleaning his bathroom and there was a quite unmistakable stain on the shower door at waist level. In deference to the more delicate listener, he had committed the sin of Onan and left it for me to find. I would like to say this was my "come to Jesus moment," as it were. But actually it was a few weeks afterward, when a client mentioned casually to my boss that she preferred an organic service to the more traditional because it was a relief to her to be dealing with members of her socioeconomic class. At home I reevaluated my position. I did not love these assholes, and did not want to clean their stupid tacky houses. I couldn't continue being a spectator of the pity parade of my life, I had a destiny, and it was time to get serious about it; I would not be defined by the dramatic departure of all the men in my life. I was inseminated with purpose! As it were.

Then I got a call from New York.

It was a woman I'd worked for prior to Hogwarts. She had just taken a position as culture editor of an "aspirational" Condé Nast fashion and lifestyle magazine whose key demographic was single urban women with a median annual income of $103,000. Within a year I was a contributing editor. The last thing I'll claim is that the experience did have its charms. I'm still a girl. The effervescent closing minutes of a gala in a dress you could never afford when the ties and morals become looser, models in the background smiling with too much gum like the children they are, or being the girl reporter sent to disarm famous men, the way their brains short-circuit when you turn them down. Not that I mean to exaggerate how frequently I turned them down. I took secret pleasure in passing through the housing projects on my way to the East River promenade to run; the men in athletic jerseys two sizes too large and women in painted-on jeans with behinds so protuberant it seemed like they had to be inflated a reminder of the street my mother lived on, the unrecognition in all of their faces that we had anything in common. I attempted to justify this life by remembering that Joan Didion had worked for *Vogue* and gone on to great success and great love. Of course, Sylvia Plath had also worked for *Mademoiselle*...

Had there ever been such an ingrate? Yes, I was aware that any job in the existing journalistic climate was like a fairy tale, let alone at a print monthly. No, it did not escape me that this was the archetypal dream job of a romantic comedy protagonist. But history was repeating, Terry. The city was a perpetually self-altering maze of DISTRACTION: who can get in where and where happens to be worth getting into at the moment and who hates who—which is easy enough to keep track of because everyone hates everyone, though for reasons mysterious. (The reason is always jealousy.) But you persist through this byzantine web of snubbing and status anxiety based on nothing but ephemeral patterns of condensation and the reason is the party, not even the party itself, the line to the party and the promise it implies of better fashion, better people, better intoxicants (please). The fact that it will simply be populated by the same people making the same migration is missing the point. And, of course, the line is only an advertisement because it's not like you'll be standing in it like some loser.

However, for all that amused about this life—and only the worst prig would pretend it's unamusing—there was one problem: it didn't belong to me. This person who had just hours ago stumbled home to throw away the ripped stockings and scrub off the smeared mascara of the night before, who was now wearing a Roberto Cavalli skirt of a certain length because she would be appearing in the "leg shot" of a third-tier morning show segment, and riding in the elevator with gazelle-like women smiling their hatred while behind each other's backs they posted unflattering pictures of each other online—this person was a double, the changeling of Galvan family lore. She was as far from the person I was supposed to be as the maid in Texas cleaning up some kinesiology major's come stain. I was helpless, the victim of an identity thief I was always chasing, but never fast enough or clever enough or, in my heart, prepared enough, to catch.

One night I was at a book party with the changeling's friends—young, striving journalism types, most of whom worked for publications devoted to less frivolous fields than her own. But to tell the truth, Terry, I believe that most journalism is fashion journalism. It's a sea of flume: au courant opinions and half-formed analysis as rigorous as cocktail party chatter, the educated gliding on the winds of their own pontification. I came to call them—and make no mistake I lumped myself in this—"the Bitterati." Because everyone in the circle was a frustrated something else; their unwritten novels and screenplays kindling for their enmity for Malcolm Gladwell or Jonathan Franzen, anyone whose success was more comfortable to malign than attempt to emulate. Sometimes I would end up drunkenly in their beds without letting them touch me to amuse myself. Sad satellite males, not a real man in the bunch.

The party was being held at a certain ostentatious hotel penthouse bar that may or may not have been cool at that point, but it was irrelevant to me because the waitresses were golden sylphs who glissaded across the floor without their feet touching the ground and the bathrooms with black reflective tiling and floor-to-ceiling windows overlooking the water were designed for licentious abuses, and such imperial disdain for taste and restraint was irresistible to the Diane in me. That night a storm was coming. There was a bank of black cloud over Jersey City like a single ominous protozoa. It felt like the wake for a god. At our table after the customary Franzenfreude, the conversation turned to a recent David Brooks article. A frequent contributor to the *Times' Book Review*, Brooks adopted a posture of sort of Oscar Wilde superiority and announced that evolutionary biology was the "phrenology of the twenty-first century." He expounded on his umbrage: the nerve of biologists trying to usurp the province of artists and philosophers. This line of reasoning has a name: Human Exceptionalism. Essentially this is the belief that while there is no God, human beings have preferential status in an otherwise random universe, thus giving the educated permission to worship themselves. I recalled something I had picked up from random reading, that the physical structure of the neuron is no different than lightning or a tree; an ideal form for the flow of energy— something so beautiful it had to be true. I did not contribute this to a conversation taking the absence of God as a given. I was supposed to be an observer, my art concerned what was eternally true, and here I was caught in a maze whose existence was defined by being different than it was the week before, on what was in fashion to hate. Of course I had once argued fiercely with Harry for espousing the scientific school it now depressed me so completely to hear dismissed, but any argument has way more to do with your feelings toward the arguer than whatever is actually coming out of his mouth. And this time I did not argue back, I let a learned fool publically dismiss the mysteries closest to my own heart to not appear frivolous. I wrote about OLFACTORY EMPIRES and THE POWER OF PINK in an office place with a designated "Crying Room"—what could I say without sounding like SUCH A GIRL? I was taken most seriously when listening to men listen to themselves.

The clouds descended, consuming the opposing cityscape entirely except for a dim red light from the W Hotel providing a Fitzgerald homage. A woman joined our group, an old undergraduate friend of one of the Bitterati stopping by to stay hello. She was a movie producer visiting from Los Angeles, a pretty blonde woman of the type that I'm normally disposed to hate on sight. I may not have been enamored of my company at the time but I certainly didn't want my monopoly on their attention disrupted by a blonde, leggy Californian. However, she was one of those unusually socially adept women who knew when she was being perceived as a threat and responded to it by courting the woman who felt that way and putting her at ease. As it happened the conversation between us was effortless, transitioning smoothly between our delight in the latest political sexting scandal and favorite highlights from Joyce Carol Oates' Twitter feed and professing polite jealousy of each other's accessories and bodies. We began discussing a recent think piece on *Slate* regarding that keystone of modern feminine anxiety over whether a woman can "play by a man's rules." She sighed with exhaustion that this was still subject to debate: the world was filled with countless examples of women who were perfectly fulfilled by their achievements and were having too much fun to notice if their happiness was incomplete by society's standards. I was happy to pretend to agree with her, as if I personally knew an abundance of such women, as if my thirtieth birthday was not approaching and this question never kept me up at night. She didn't have long to stay before her next engagement, so we exchanged cards. Her smile flickered when she looked at mine. Under ordinary circumstances this would have been enough to drive me to the edge of persecution fantasies, but she carried herself with such warmth and maturity that I convinced myself I was seeing things.

After she left, her friend from our group proceeded to explain to us her unfortunate romantic situation. Apparently she had invited a charmless younger man to live with her, everyone but her seeing him as having the social graces of a baboon. This wearied me. She was so pleasant and well put together and her legs were up to my chin—what did it mean if she was as hopeless as the rest of us? More details emerged about the sad cliché she was caught in: the boor in question was a screenwriter (at which there were knowing scoffs, though half present had a partial draft of a screenplay lying around somewhere) who came from Austin (more knowing scoffs) and dressed like he'd walked off a community theater production of *Midnight Cowboy*.

I stared for a while into the clouds across the water, then excused myself. I walked to the subway. It was summer and the air was rank and sweet with the garbage bags piled on the sidewalks. Steam drifted up from grates in the sidewalk, and a busboy walked down stairs cut directly into the sidewalk. This image always appealed to me, like the pavement was made of water. Distracted, I bumped into an old homeless man sitting in a wheelchair. His pants were bunched around his knees as though he was sitting on the toilet. The combination of my horror at having collided with a crippled homeless person and the grotesque comedy of his appearance, his pale, shrunken genitals, caused a burst of defenseless laughter to escape my mouth. He howled like a banshee, the way people do when their high is disrupted: *Who are you to laugh at ME-E-E-E! Who are you to laugh at MY BO-O-O-O-ODY!* I hurried down the sidewalk to the next avenue, telling myself to concentrate more on my feet than my pity. Distracted, I came within inches of stepping into the path of a bus. The wind of it swept my bangs aside. On the subway, my car pulled abreast of another one on a parallel track, you know how it is when for a couple of seconds, you have a perfectly clear view of the train next to yours and there is something inscrutably cosmic about the experience, like some vignette out of the *Tibetan Book of the Dead*. I hoped I would see sex, or a murder. There was an elderly Asian man standing in the other car. He was wearing a dark overcoat though it was summer. He reached into his overcoat and flung several white shapes to the roof of the car. They were white paper butterflies. As they descended he reached into his coat again and produced a fan, which he waved back and forth, causing the wings of the butterflies to flap. They ascended once more, circling each other. Then the other track dipped and that train went down another tunnel and out of view and there was just the reflection of a drunk girl crying. Distracted, I wound up at the door of one of the members of the Bitterati. Lying in bed later that night he asked in earnest what I was doing. He had known me from my old days in the city and saw it, the thing inside myself I was flailing so wildly to prevent anyone from noticing. The next morning, I hid my panties in his bedding without telling him; his girlfriend was an editor of a Brooklyn literary magazine who had acted superior to me at the last Nick Denton party.

It was around then I started fabricating. The first time was innocent enough: I quoted a source as saying something that when I checked my notes for the exact wording there was no record of. This puzzled me until I realized—it was not something this person had actually said, but something I wished she had. I filed it as it was. Call it the frustrated novelist's revenge. Call it petulance. In the months before the piece ran I was a wreck with anxiety. Right alongside my stupid pride over this dizzyingly pointless defiance was the child's dread of getting caught. I never was. My artistic ambition expanded shortly: fabricating whole scenarios and characters. "Fabulist." It had a certain ring to it. I convinced myself there was a nobility to fabulism the same as there was servitude. Certainly a thrill. As my folio increased, so did my dread. I had vivid fantasies of being escorted from the office through a corridor of whispers; not being able to eat in public without feeling the incriminating stares. My face flushed at the thought. It was the highlight of my day.

Finally, the woman who originally brought me to the magazine requested to meet me for a drink under clandestine circumstances. The blood drained from my fingers, I sailed to our appointment in a state of grace. *Finally*! She told me the magazine was folding and requested an up-to-date copy of my CV—she knew of a position opening at *The Cut*. I gave her the CV and blew off the interview. The magazine went under and I celebrated my unemployment with denial, changing nothing about my lifestyle. But the maze reconfigured around me; I did not come from a family and no longer had the institutional backing of Mr. Nast, and, not so gradually, I could no longer get a table at this restaurant or breeze through the door of this club. Inevitably, that same penthouse bar became my staple; my inner Diane would always have a place there, like *Cheers* or *The Shining*, and by the end I was going there almost every night. This wound up being counterproductive: in spite of my declining status there was always some venture capitalist who had briefly been a lit major in undergraduate who would cover the bill and occasionally propose marriage. Women who believe that men prefer dumb and hot to smart and hot are probably neither smart enough or hot enough. Men will always want to possess what they fear they can't. The changeling would never lack opportunities. But it's commonplace that you don't change until it's time to change; by now I couldn't tell the difference between a party and a bunch of geese honking at each other, and I had grown bored wrecking myself on shoals of cock. Not to mention what was now a small mountain of credit card debt. A creditor actually beeped in while I was on the phone with my father telling him I needed help.

And that, Terry, is how you came to have this imaginary conversation with a grown woman living in her father's basement in Pittsburgh. That is how I came to fuck up my life this much.

✦

All grays pale next to southwestern Pennsylvania in winter; it is the gray caked to the paneling of a dark car that seems unwashable, like an innate feature of the car itself. The men in Carhartt jackets with complexions like the car paneling, ruddy-faced and thick-wristed teenagers going to vocational colleges, girls with nail art and striped hair extensions. I was suffocated with repulsion and heartbreak. I would have offered up every particle of my being to save them and given anything to not be around them. People would ask if I was HERE TO STAY and I would coyly say WE'LL SEE as if I had some trick up my sleeve other than deflecting my humiliation. I got dinner with a cousin my age, having to suggest a restaurant that was not TGI Fridays. She lived in a neighboring county with her husband and two young children and worried about the quality of the school district. I asked why they didn't move closer to the city and she looked at me like a Martian. She had two kids and her husband was laid off. She called me "Moneybags" and looked at me with the suspicion that many local women did, that I considered myself to be an alien visitor, that I wasn't voicing what a stuck-up bitch I actually was. The suspicion with which my mother would have looked at me if she met me today, the snob she had dreamed into existence. The worst kind of snob: a failed one. I ran into an ex at the 7-Eleven who was opportunistic enough to believe this was an opening; I deflected, suggesting he find me on Facebook, only to be informed he couldn't currently afford Internet access because of his child support situation. I began running again like I had not since Austin. But Austin summers are hot and wet and louche and Pittsburgh winters call to mind the vision from Norse eschatology of a wolf swallowing the sun, so it felt like I needed it to: grim survival. This feeling appealed to me so much I would wear my running clothes when I went to bed and be up and on the streets while it was still dark, just the sound of my breath and the horn of a coal train. This ensured there would be some motion in my life; otherwise I could spend minutes on end staring at a Diet Coke before sipping it.

Jack Kelly was equally stymied by the fact of my existence each time he was confronted with it. My long-suffering stepmother had finally left him and he had become so set in his ways he derived more satisfaction from the conviction no woman could understand him than he could from the understanding of a woman. And he'd developed the hoarding instinct common to the obstinately lonely—acquiring whatever junk from thrift stores and yard sales to create a consoling fortress of clutter to best recreate their inner state. In opposition to our respective dynamics with my mother there had always been a cold strain between us, but epic rows erupted over this junk; I challenged him on the utility of a foam cushion with no casing or for that matter a piece of furniture to go with it or an intricate lamp made of popsicle sticks that didn't actually function as a lamp, his defense was what a bargain they had been—given the current state of my finances perhaps I could take a lesson. But what truly stunned about the relationship was its perfect symbiosis. He treated me like an egg whose safekeeping he had been assigned by some highly ironic cosmic pedagogue and I cleaned his house.

Soon enough he recruited me for his pub trivia team. Though I had started attending meetings of my benevolent cult, I needed some kind of activity other than running; my father made sure there was always a Diet Coke in front of me, and by the end of the night I would be caffeinated to the point of trembling. I don't have much to contribute to the literature of sobriety except that you discover the miraculous truth of every platitude you've ever heard and that in the cold light of biochemistry it means experiencing every single moment of every single day (excluding, naturally, the number of SSRIs and the antianxiety medication I was taking). He just needed someone who knew popular culture. All my life I'd had a child's veneration of my father's intellect. He may have possessed little aptitude for converting it into material gain, but the sheer volume of information as un-triaged as the yard sale items he was acquiring had been a source of pride for me in a *my dad can beat up your dad* sort of way. It was also his only quality that my mother uniformly spoke highly of. She liked to say I'd inherited his brain and her balls. So it came as no small surprise to discover he cheated at pub trivia; discreetly eavesdropping on other teams when stumped, or filling in answers after pencils were down. His team had long been champions, and this Machiavellian commitment to victory in an environment with this low of stakes made me unexpectedly proud. It was nice to know there was some winner's edge in my blood.

✦

MY FIRST MEETING I walked past the door three times. I had to employ the athlete's trick of visualizing myself walking through the door to finally go through with it. I sat by myself. Young women who avoid processed foods are not in large supply at meetings, and I thought if I looked haughty enough it would mask how afraid I was. It didn't, and people smiled and said hello without making a federal case of it. The banality of redemption. One woman near me told a story to her friend about how annoyed she was her email had been hacked because of all the typos in the spam attributed to her. Another blue-collar archetype sighed to his friend he wasn't getting younger, nobody is. I wondered if anyone in the room had partied with my mom. We read a passage from the Big Book, something about how going to prison opened a door. There was no blinding epiphany or anything like that, it's more like...like candles on a winter night. Just knowing that you are not the only one in the dark is enough, maybe. But that's between you and the God of your understanding.

This group met in a black box theater. Diane would have appreciated that.

✦

OF COURSE I THOUGHT about her. This was not New York, things did not change here; there were moments when the past bled through the page more strongly than the present. The smell of onions and pierogies on the griddle in a restaurant, the rhythm of bumps crossing over a bridge, the gasp of cold air opening a freezer door in the grocery store—it was hard to predict what would cause the unfurling of some Proustian apparition that would trigger the desire to dive into the nearest bottle. I meditated on the irony that it was Diane who had inspired in me the faith in destiny and that even from beyond the grave was the most likely to derail it. It made me feel closer to her; I was sure she was on a cloud somewhere pleased with the dramatic tension. I prayed for the clarity to distinguish the desire for a drink and the need for one and, for all I know, she helped answer it.

✦

MY ABSTINENCE INCLUDED MEN as well as alcohol. There was no shortage of housecleaning to be done. However, one development around this time was Mark resurfacing. For several years he had been living in New York and working for Tribeca Productions, but he would be leaving before long because he'd finally cobbled together financing for the feature he'd been working on back when we were together. It pleased me that Jason and Harry were wrong: they had perceived Mark as a loser in the same way they perceived all less predatory creatures. As if any man who spent less than every hour of the day obsessing over how powerful he was could hardly be entitled to the same oxygen supply, let alone to come into his own in his own time. Yet it was also bittersweet to feel that I possessed the Midas vagina: destined to lose men before they became something. (My resentments were well fed by the martyr's conviction that this was a larger cosmic scheme of persecution as opposed to the result of simple decisions made by myself.)

At any rate, we had remained friends and met for the occasional lunch during my time in the city, but he had been in a relationship with a sweet girl who supported his ambitions without being overly burdened with her own. I was genuinely pleased for him: Mark had found a Mark! But that had recently run its course and we were talking again often, sometimes for hours. The sound of his voice was logical and comforting, and my local sponsor, while as well-intentioned as could be, harbored too much of a girl crush on me to hold me accountable. She was a waitress who had never lived more than a few miles from the home of her birth and had read every issue of the late magazine of my employment and her head swam at the idea that I had lived in a world that she thought was a fantasy invented for grocery checkout counters. Mark saw through my prevarications and, though his nature was no more confrontational than it had been since we were together, now when my actions or my own interpretations of my actions started to spiral he would just chuckle tolerantly and say, "Okay, Lee." And then I could laugh too, a small vacation from hating myself from the vantage of his tolerant amusement, the creeping sense that I might actually deserve it. Forgiveness. *Okay, Lee.*

Then he mentioned he was going to the Sundance Film Festival, they'd be putting him up in a halfway decent hotel. As his end was covered, he could float me the airfare, no sweat when I paid him back. I was quiet.

"I mean this in as casual a way as I can," he said.

I said I'd think about it. Head and heart were at yet another impasse. You can't go back again, that's not how growth works. Conditions change, and you can't attempt to recreate a set of preexisting conditions as though the same design flaw isn't there. But…suppose conditions change to permit the emergence of new conditions. This chiding, knowing Mark, the Mark who FINISHED THINGS, was not the Mark of the past, and for the first time in my life I was sincere about getting well—the creeping sense that I deserved it. Of course this could just as easily have been an argument made from fear and because it was cold. The instant I believed I had reached some kind of clarity, breath fogged the window. I was now thirty years old, and had more than once made the threat in the past that if I reached this age unmarried and unpublished I would throw myself under a train. I knew Mark was a good man, and was sad to imagine the leggy, deserving blonde woman on the other coast with a young, Texan time bomb in her bed, and the good men in her past she hadn't settled for believing she was happy playing a man's game.

Settling.

Even now with my fortunes at their lowest and his at their peak, I viewed Mark as settling. Was it possible my entire twenties were just a dress rehearsal for the same mistakes to happen again and again? Was it possible in light of my entire twenties to dismiss a man I knew would be a good father?

There was another consideration.

The reason so many writers are drinkers is simply because drinking and writing are both ways to manage the darkness. Now I had stopped drinking, leaving no choice between the terror and the work. I had gotten back to it, my real work, for the first time in years. I was like Victor Hugo locked nude in a room with only paper and pencil. Was that Hugo or Dumas? Or entirely apocryphal? Irrelevant. There was no man in my life, no piece to file, no romance with my own destruction.

I had no more distractions.

✦

THINGS ARE GETTING OUT of hand. What does any of this have to do with YOU?

The objective of this letter is to accept responsibility, repay debts, and ask forgiveness.

I should not have said I didn't love you anymore. Recently a cousin posted the Christian the Lion video on her Facebook and it was the version where at the moment the lion runs up and hugs those guys it plays "I Will Always Love You" and it would have taken a forklift to lift me up.

Your first movie is about to come out. I hear it's pretty bad. You and the director fought like cats and dogs. I am not worried about you. This life is not for the faint of heart, and I know your heart is an endurable piece of meat. I hear you break hearts. (*Of course,* I have gathered far more intelligence on your activities than these pages reflect.) The party line of my gender is to vilify a man who is cavalier with the female heart without necessarily excavating why he became this way. But I know you are the wound you are because of me and, like the sick bitch Pygmalion I am trying not to be, it gives me a sense of accomplishment.

I should not have said I didn't love you anymore.

I remember the morning you left. The bright spring sun and the sound of the grackles. You sitting hunched on my stoop, your back as lean as a two-by-four, and seemingly as brittle. Your truck in the gravel lot with an oversize army navy duffel bag in the back, pretty much everything you owned. I was on a lot of pills, but had the presence of mind to grab Zion by the collar and prevent his escape. You made a comment about the price of dog-skin boots. I sat next to you and would have liked to have rubbed your back, but even I was not cruel enough to comfort you.

The look in your eyes. As a gifted youth of course you had chafed at the notion that you would have a superior appreciation of art with maturity, but only now did you finally understand the majority of the country and western corpus, or the book of Genesis. Could it be true? Could it be true I had fallen out of love with you just like that? You did not ask because you were too tender to hear me repeat the lie.

Of course it was a fucking lie!

Why did you have to believe me? Why did you have to leave?

I touched your shoulder and you flinched. I said you should get a back rub before the drive. You asked if I was offering you a fuck. I told you I didn't want to do that. You observed that mine was the species of self-sabotage that caused the maximum level of inconvenience for others.

"I'm so proud of you," I said.

"I guess you can take it and shove it up your ass," you said.

I listened to the grackles. This sound didn't occur around Harry's house. He shot all the grackles with an air rifle and now they stayed away.

You stood.

"There is a light in you that can change lives," he said. "And no one is trying to destroy it more than you. Enjoy becoming your mother."

My face was hot with weeping I had not noticed. I stumbled to my knees and clung to you, shaking and burying my face into your abdomen.

I should not have said I didn't love you anymore.

"Go," I said.

✦

THE THING IS, IF this letter serves its purpose, if I really and truly seek forgiveness for the way that I wronged you, the thing that follows that is—

I don't need you. I quit drinking because it was time to quit drinking. I started working again because enough already. I am a cockroach. I am Diana Ross. I am in the slow, arduous, intensely uncinematic process of not becoming my mother, and I need a man to save me like I need a hole in the head.

But I miss your brain. Talking with you was like a sandbox of infinite dimension, infinite joy in what it could become. You are the broken angel who brought my worst self to light, an exorcism in recursive loop. You are my favorite person in the world, and more audacious than forgiveness, I want to feel your hand on the back of my neck again. I want to feel the tip of your finger on my broken thumbnail. I want to feel like you have the longest, greediest arms, holding me all to yourself. I want to feel that you are proud of me. You are the mythologist that became the defining myth of my heart, and actually setting my pen aside, abandoning all flights and digressions and epistolary tap dancing and actually sending this means—

It means—

There is nothing more to say.

SHE SITS FOR A long time looking at her computer screen. She hits Return twice and types:

Goodbye,

Me

She hits Command+P. There is no reason to go over the document one more time—at this point doing so would be grounds for calling her sponsor.

She rises from the desk and sits Indian-style on the bed. The bed is really a mattress on the basement floor. The floor is carpeted. The only natural light comes from a narrow window close to the ceiling. Her father painted the walls turquoise to liven things up for her, but he couldn't be bothered to get painter's tape so at the floor and ceiling there is a border of hodgepodge rectangle edges from the roller and then the base color.

She reaches for her phone on the nightstand, which is a milk crate with a lamp on it. The lamp is made out of popsicle sticks; her father got it at a thrift store for three dollars. She opens a text message she has been avoiding for too long. It is from Mark.

Verdict?

Her hope has been that the right answer would simply emerge, but every time she has decided on one she has been overwhelmed with panic that it is the wrong one. Maybe there isn't a right answer. It could be that this sense that the next decision she makes will irrevocably alter the course of her life can be attributed to generalized anxiety morbidly fixating on this specific issue. It could be that what she does next is not meaningful at all in the scheme of things, that this indecision is worse than whatever she could decide, that if she is taking things ONE DAY AT A TIME what could be the harm in being a little less lonely for a weekend. Could feeling a man's hands touching her with love really be worse than another night of reading Flannery O'Connor to a lamp made of popsicle sticks? She tells herself to relax, her stomach to unknot, this is not the thing that knocks the world from its axis. More importantly, this is not GOING BACK AGAIN. Life is a labyrinth, not a maze—every step you take is just one more that brings you closer to the center.

She looks over at the stack of pages incrementally rising on the printer. She pulls the sleeves of her cardigan over her fingers the way that used to give her comfort as a child wearing adult clothes, and rests her elbows on her knees and her chin on her knuckles. Abruptly she gets up and stands in front of the mirror, where she slips off her cardigan and lifts her shirt. She bends and removes her yoga pants and then her underwear. She picks up the phone and hits the button to respond to his message with a photo, standing white, a frantic, amphibious white like some cave life form, blind and primordial and stupidly innocent.

Every step you take is just one more that bring you closer to the center. Or whatever story you tell yourself. Thank you and goodbye.

Goodbye.

Goodbye.

Goodbye.

She is just about to send this picture as her response when there is the sound of the front door buzzer. She pulls her clothes back on and goes upstairs and opens the door. She wheels back several steps and leans against the newel. Her hand covers her mouth, but she makes no sound.

I... I... I... I'm sorry, Terry, I need a moment.

"I love you, you bitch," said Jason